# Mongol Healer

## A Novel

Regina L. Wei

The Wei of Healing, LLC

Published by The Wei of Healing, LLC

www.healingwei.com

ISBN 979-8-9947897-2-8 (Paperback)

ISBN 979-8-9947897-6-6 (Hardcover)

ISBN 979-8-9947897-8-0 (E-book)

Cover design by Olga Norman

Cover art by Leilani Norman

*For my parents:*
*Words cannot express the deep love and gratitude I feel for you. Your lives are a testament to the power of compassion, generosity, and wisdom in action. You have provided me with a moral compass that always points true, and I am honored to carry on our ancestral legacy of teaching and healing.*

*I also dedicate this work to the spirit of Inanna Rising and to all the Wise Woman healers who form the hollow bone through which healing flows to this hurting world.*

*Finally, this work is for you: may you receive the healing that is in this book, and may your journey be deeply supported.*

Proceeds from this novel support **Inanna Rising's Patient Equity Scholarship Fund** which expands access to psychedelic-assisted therapy. The fund helps to ensure that more people can experience the healing made possible when we work with reverence and care alongside sacred medicines.

More information is available at **InannaRising.org**.

# Contents

# The Fledgling



Wú steps out into the courtyard and gazes straight into the face of a brilliant morning sun. Beijing is usually cloaked in sulfurous smog so clear autumn skies are rare, but the air is especially clean today after last night's storm. It smells like rain-soaked soil, and the early morning sky holds promises of a deep Mongolian blue. Wú spends a few moments looking directly at the sun, swaying a little in the light and warmth. This has been her practice for over a quarter of a century.

Something needs her attention. A fledgling at her feet whose flight feathers are almost fully formed: mouth gaping open, it draws breath after laborious breath. The lines of its small body are angular with youth while large eyes in a fuzzy head are wide with fear and innocence. It is very late in the season for fledglings. In a few weeks all the swallows will be flying south for the winter, but it is likely this one's parents had to rebuild a fallen or plundered nest.

Adult swallows circle overhead, weaving the fabric of their community with staccato chirps in counterpoint, tails scissoring in hairpin turns. They call to their little one, but when it strains to reply, its cries are lost to the vastness of the blue sky.

Every spring, swallows come to nest in the low eaves of Wú's simple dwelling, but even more nest among the bright red rafters of her neighbor's grand, newly renovated two-story home. Her neighbor has now taken his father's old title of Master Zhu and has made quite a name for himself as a qigong master. They grew up as next-door neighbors in adjacent compounds, but their paths have diverged widely since they were children more than half a century ago. Wú does not mind that the swallows prefer his grand home to her humble one. She watches them every morning as they swoop through the air above his courtyard calling to each other. Very social creatures, swallows. They never fly alone.

Wú sinks into a squat next to the fledgling and holds her hands over the tiny body. Relaxing her fingers, she breathes deeply and immediately feels the tingle of healing energy as it flows from her palms to the small bird. Once again, she raises her gaze to focus on the face of that very dear and familiar friend, the sun. Dozens of swallows wing wide arcs high above.

After some time, she moves her hands away and sees that the fledgling's breath has become calmer and more regular. The heavily lidded eyes droop in rest as it lies still, rousing occasionally to reposition a wing or gently shake its head.

Wú watches the slow rise and fall of its breath for a few moments then sighs. She wonders if it will survive the day. Seeing that the small grassy patch where it lies will soon be in the shade, she leaves the bird where it fell during the night. So it goes: what the night offers the day claims, and what the day offers the night claims.

She takes hold of her market basket and slips a small cloth purse into her pocket. The fruit sellers are selling the last of the summer peaches, and she is craving some of their sweetness this morning. One can still find the hefty, firm-fleshed, northern peaches she grew up with, but now there are also the juicy, tender, and sweeter southern varieties. They are so sweet it is like eating golden candy.

Peaches were a luxury when she was young. On the rare occasion her father brought home a small basket of peaches, a gift from one of his students or a colleague, Wú carefully cradled the fruit in her palms and stroked the fuzz that was as soft as a baby bird's breast. In the evening, after they finished dinner, she soaked a peach in very hot water before transferring it to very cold water. After the hot and cold water soaks, the skin peeled off easily. A single peach was carefully divided into thin slices to be offered to her grandmother first and then to her father. Life was simple then.

Wú pauses for a moment before leaving the compound as she senses the movement of different energies within herself this morning: the long hairs of a horse's tail wafting gently windward; mournful notes of nomadic song; the slip of sun-faded silk against her fingertips. The first time she tasted a peach on the Inner Mongolian grassland, a gift from a friend who rarely smiled but who showed his caring in small ways. Things never revisited much less spoken of after so many years. It is odd, this new movement of old things, like a gentle stirring at the bottom of a vast lake where things have lain undisturbed for countless eons. It has been so long since she has thought about her old life, but if things are rising to the surface now, she will welcome them.

Wú opens the door to the alley and sees a young woman standing outside, very young, mid-20s. Her long, dyed-orange hair is windblown and in need of a good brushing. Wú sees in the young woman's eyes that she seeks something but does not know what she is looking for. She looks exhausted. Wú also carried a lot of pain at one time. Her heart softening, she suddenly understands why these old things have risen to the surface: the young woman has come so Wú can share her story of healing with her.

"You don't know me. I don't want to disturb you," the young woman begins to say, but Wú waves away the apology. Stepping back into the compound, she invites the young woman in with a smile.

# The Struggle Session


MY LIFE AS A Red Guard truly began when I burned all of my father's books on a smoldering August day in 1966. He did not see me carry armful after armful of his books, notebooks, and letters out into the courtyard because he was being reformed at a hard labor camp in Inner Mongolia. Only when I saw all of his things piled up and ready for the match did I realize the full extent of his love affair with the West: textbooks, novels, biographies, thin volumes of poetry, postcard-sized prints of famous works of European art. He had collected and kept anything and everything that was of or from the bourgeois West, but his scholarship and writings posed a direct threat to my future. It gave me great pleasure to see it all thrown into a chaotic jumble on the ground: pages upon pages of his neat, scholarly handwriting crushed under the weight of books flung open in wanton abandon; dozens of notebooks that documented decades of thought and research smudged with dirt. It was counter-revolutionary trash destined for the purifying flames of the revolution.

As I surveyed my father's things, I smoothed the front of my new Red Guard uniform: crisp military lines, wide leather belt with a heavy copper buckle, and a red armband with the characters for Red Guard written in yellow. A postcard-sized print caught my eye, and I hesitated for the space of a breath. It had been my favorite, a mother and daughter self-portrait painted by Élisabeth-Louise Vigée-Le Brun, a woman whose talents had caught the attention of France's doomed nobility in the 18th Century. Father had kept the print under a sheet of glass on his desk along with his other important letters and papers. As a child, I often climbed into his chair when he was away teaching and gazed at the image until I had memorized every detail. Maybe it was the way the girl, embracing her mother's neck, twisted her head around to look at us with an expression both sweet and sultry for we had caught her in an intimate moment with her mother. The painter herself was the picture of Western bohemian beauty with her messy curly locks and creamy white skin. Her dress, made of a light, gauzy material that hugged her full figure, fell open at the top to reveal the flawless, pale skin of her shapely shoulders and arms. A red scarf embroidered with gold thread casually held the dress together at the waist while a robe the color of green tea slipped languorously down her back and across her lap: a mother in all her lovely voluptuousness. She was the mother I never had.

I shook my head and threw back my uniformed shoulders: it was a decadent, bourgeois beauty that would burn well at the top of that large pile of foreign and forbidden things. I touched several matches to the mound that came up to my chest and watched as words and images were haltingly then quickly consumed by flames. Soon, the bonfire was throwing off so much heat that it pushed me back against the dusty brick wall of the courtyard.

My heart beat quickly as I watched the books burn, the smoke causing me to squint. All the memories that I had of my father were of him bent over his work at the desk, his glasses glinting in the candlelight when he moved his head. When I was much younger, he sometimes invited me to pull up a low stool next to his chair and read to me from his books printed in foreign languages. Although I did not understand his love for Wordsworth, Byron, Keats, Hugo, Flaubert, Goethe, Balzac, and so many more, at such times I was like a blossom turning its face to the sun because that was when he came alive. I still remembered a smattering of the English and French phrases he had taught me.

As I watched the books burn, my eyes were dry but a deep ache pulsated in my chest and crept into my throat. My breath was shallow and fast as if there was a tight band around my ribcage. My father would be devastated if he knew what I, his own daughter, had done. He would not understand that I was helping him by destroying those feudal things.

I do not know how long I stood pressed against the rough wall watching the fire before I remembered that I was a soldier of the revolution. There were things I needed to do that day. It was my duty to press on.

There came a rapid, heavy pounding on our compound door, and I heard a familiar voice: "Comrade Wú! Open the door! The struggle session for Zhū Shǒuliàng has begun already at the school. What is keeping you? The Revolutionary Committee is taking roll!"

I roused myself and quickly unlatched the door for Xiǎomèi, a fellow Red Guard. Like me, Xiǎomèi was dressed in a khaki-colored uniform and her shoulder-length hair was plaited into two, no-nonsense braids like mine. Though she was in a class two years lower than mine in school, we had always been close—we had both lost our mothers when we were too young to remember. As Xiǎomèi surveyed the fire in the courtyard, I quickly moved around the study to conceal the fact that I had just emptied all the bookshelves. After a moment's thought, I opened my well-worn copy of Chairman Máo's quotations to page 28 and placed it prominently in the center of the desk:

> *A revolution is not a dinner party, or writing an essay,*
> *or painting a picture, or doing embroidery; it cannot be*
> *so refined, so leisurely and gentle, so temperate, kind,*
> *courteous, restrained and magnanimous.*

*A revolution is an insurrection, an act of violence by
which one class overthrows another.*

As always, the Chairman's words gave me courage. The
exhilaration of the revolution filling my chest, I lined up the
*Collected Works of Máo* on the center shelf where the vermillion
volumes would catch the eye of anyone who entered. I glanced
around the room one more time. The shelves looked bare and
forlorn without my father's books. I hurried outside.

Out in the courtyard, Xiǎomèi shook her head as she circled
the dying fire, the glowing edges of hundreds of charred pages still
discernible among the embers. "Well done," she said. "It is wise of
you to distance yourself from his black past. Today you will distance
yourself from your neighbor, that charlatan Zhū Shǒuliàng!"

It did not take us long to reach the school where the struggle
session was being held. The large, four-story building where we
attended classes had been completely transformed in the few weeks
after schools closed so students could join the revolution. Virtually
every wall was plastered from floor to ceiling with big-character
posters: searing critiques of members of the community. Posters
fluttered from all sides as we hurried past, and glimpses into the open
doors of classrooms revealed even more posters on the blackboards
and even plastered over windows. The smell of newsprint, ink and
glue mingled with the smoke that lingered on my uniform and in my
hair. In the main hallways, for lack of wall space, posters had been
strung right across the walkway like lines of ink-stained laundry. The
thin newsprint fluttered and grazed the tops of our caps as Xiǎomèi
and I ducked to avoid the vehement denunciations.

Although my Red Guard comrades and I had penned quite a
few of the critiques ourselves, I did not in that moment feel the pride
or righteousness of the revolution because I was thinking about

the last time I spoke with my neighbor Zhū Shǒuliàng, whom we respectfully called Shīfu, because of his status as one of the most esteemed and beloved qigong masters in all of Beijing. How things can change in two years.

It had been a very hot and humid summer day not unlike the one on which the struggle session was held. My father was away teaching, and I went next door to the qigong master's compound after I had bound my breasts with a long strip of undyed cotton cloth. As I had done hundreds of times before, I let myself in through the double front doors, always unlocked, and stepped over the high threshold into the outer courtyard. Our adjoining compounds had once been a part of a large *sìhéyuàn* that belonged to a wealthy merchant family before the Liberation. Our quarters had formed part of the *xīxiàngfáng*, the west wing, while Shīfu's compound contained the original inner and outer courtyards, the main house, and the east wing. While our small courtyard consisted of the walled-off side entrance to the original complex, Shīfu's outer courtyard had a *chuíhuā* gate that opened onto the larger inner courtyard where he taught his private pupils. The outer courtyard was lined with large, potted peony and jasmine plants. The peonies had finished blooming several weeks ago, but the air was sweet with the jasmine's fragrance. I bent down to sniff a cluster of blossoms and felt the small, star-shaped petals tickle the tip of my nose.

When I went through the *chuíhuā* gate and around the spirit screen, I came upon a very familiar tableau. Shīfu, dressed in a dark blue, loose-fitting cotton tunic with a line of simple frog closures down the front, was just beginning the afternoon practice session with his eight most dedicated students who stood in two rows before him. All the boys were dressed like the Shīfu in cotton tunics, loose trousers, and soft-soled shoes. Shīfu's son Zhū Zhìxīn, thirteen years old at the time and a few years my junior, stood at the end of the first row.

I bowed to Shīfu and stood behind the last row. As usual, no one acknowledged my presence.

We began with slow breaths to center ourselves and circulate qi in the body before moving on to stretches and more rigorous movement. I had done the practice thousands of times and could do them with my eyes closed but was careful to place my feet and position my hands and limbs with complete attention because Shīfu had sharp eyes and was exacting in his instruction. Over the years, I had witnessed his prompt and merciless corrections with a bamboo staff when students were sloppy or too rigid in their stances, and students who did not demonstrate absolute commitment to the practice did not last long. Many boys had come and gone over the years, but these were the eight who had stayed.

Practice that day was focused on the dynamic forms that I enjoyed more than the static forms. Although Shīfu was known for being a great qigong healer and his teachings focused on cultivating and harnessing internal qi for healing purposes, I was more drawn to the strong practice of *gōngfu*. We drilled for hours with lunges, kicks, blocks, and punches until my light cotton shirt was wet through and my hair stuck to my forehead, but I was too immersed in the powerful and precise dance to stop and wipe away the sweat streaming down my face and into my collar. I was an excellent scholar and a leader among my peers at school, but there was nothing I loved better than being there in the courtyard, practicing. My body felt strong and lithe, and I felt as powerful as a young tiger. My feet knew by feel every seam, crack, and slant of the gray paving stones in Shīfu's courtyard. The stand of muted-green bamboo in the southeastern corner of the courtyard and the upward stretch of the Yulan magnolias that proffered bird-shaped blossoms every spring were more familiar to me than my father's face. When we sat in meditation under the magnolia's generous green shade, the sweat drying on our faces and on our backs, I heard the bamboo's fluttering whispers and felt the slow beat of my heart. I never felt more at peace or at home than when I was in Shīfu's courtyard which is why I returned day after day.

After the other students left and his son had gone inside, I picked up a long-handled straw broom and began to sweep the courtyard as I always did after practices. Instead of going inside like usual, Shīfu stood watching me for a few minutes then waved me over. It was one of the few times in my life that he addressed me directly.

"You have been watching us for many years."

"Yes, Shīfu." I kept my gaze directed respectfully downwards. As a student leader, I was accustomed to speaking in front of hundreds during assemblies, but I felt very small standing in front of the master.

"You have been coming every day since you were just a little thing and have been practicing on your own. You have shown more devotion to the practice than my most dedicated student. You work harder than my own son."

I stared at the ground, unsure of how he felt about my constant visits and acutely aware of the fact that I had taken what had not been offered. When he was silent for a long time, I finally looked up and was relieved to see that he was not angry. The expression in his eyes was not unkind. We looked at each other for a long moment until he spoke again, and his words came as a huge blow to me. "Xiǎo Wú, on your own and without formal instruction you have achieved a certain level of physical mastery. That is an accomplishment in itself. But I never agreed to teach you, and all that you have attained has been without a teacher's guidance." He held my gaze while I fought the urge to flee.

"You have a lot to learn, but I am not the teacher to teach you. Besides," he said looking around the plain but clean courtyard in which we stood, every detail of which I knew by heart, "all this is old and outdated. Times are changing. Some day when you understand what it is you need to master we can have a conversation. But until then—if that day comes—I do not want you to come back here."

If I had not been so mortified, I would have recognized that Shīfu was praising me for my dedication. I also would have paid more attention to the hint of sadness in his voice. It is possible he foresaw that events would spiral beyond anyone's control and had a prescience that he would be among the revolution's casualties. All that I understood at the time, however, was that I was being cut off from my life's passion. Not wanting him to see me cry, I turned and ran from the courtyard.

After that day, I never returned to Shīfu's compound, and I never again practiced qigong or *gōngfu*. I reminded myself that girls are not meant to move or use our bodies the way men do, and I was destined to be a scholar like my father. I threw myself into my studies and into the political life at school and completely shut away the part of myself that had loved the power, precision, and peace of the qigong practice.

On the day I burned my father's books two years later, I no longer thought about what I considered to be a childhood dalliance, but a part of me still respected Shīfu and knew that the struggle session would be an especially difficult test of my mettle as a Red Guard. The Yellow River, birthplace of our civilization, is made up of single drops of water that taken together form one of the greatest rivers in the world. On my own, I was merely a drop of water, but when I put aside my small droplet's concerns and joined my comrades in the revolutionary work, I became a part of a powerful, unconquerable force. I could not, therefore, let personal inclinations get in the way of my commitment to the cause; sentimentality and weakness have no place in a revolution. I needed to let go of old attachments.

The struggle session was already in full swing by the time we reached the school's athletic field. As it was a particularly important session, hundreds packed the field but it was not a boisterous gathering. People spoke in restrained whispers while keeping their eyes slanted toward the stage. Brisk patriotic music and revolutionary slogans blasted from loudspeakers all around us, cutting through the oppressively humid summer air, but it was all so much a part of the fabric of our daily lives at that point that no one really listened. The loudspeaker announcements and flyers publicizing this session had made it clear that this time, *"Energetic and definitive steps will be taken towards wiping out the running dogs of capitalist roaders and sweeping away the last traces of superstition and ignorance!"* It was not until that day that I fully appreciated what "definitive steps" really meant even though I had been the one who had penned those words on a big-character poster.

Those who were being struggled against stood in a line on the stage with their hands bound behind them and their heads bowed: the school's principal, the director of administration, professors from a nearby university, and Shīfu. They wore heavy iron placards around their necks, their names crudely scrawled upside down and crossed out with big, red Xs: the condemned. From where I stood next to the stage, I could see that the twine holding the placards cut deeply into the backs of their necks.

My stomach contracted when I saw Shīfu standing there. As a qigong master, Shīfu was one of the most self-possessed, composed, and powerful people I knew: the perfect balance between stillness and action, stillness within action. Every move he made was with intention, and energy was never wasted. When I was young, there was nothing I loved better than to watch him demonstrate the graceful, flowing qigong sequences or the dynamic, energetic *gōngfu* exercises he taught his students. His body at such times became an effortless extension of Nature itself, one with the environment. Even when he stood still, Shīfu's presence was an embodiment of the energy he cultivated, and he commanded respect. Yet now, standing with his hands bound and his head bowed, he looked very vulnerable.

About a dozen Red Guards from another faction in our school stood on the stage looking smart and invincible in their olive-colored uniforms. Dominating the microphone was a seventeen-year-old Red Guard we knew from previous struggle sessions. "Chén Hóngméng," Xiǎomèi whispered to me. "Her father is an important official which is why she is so arrogant." Chén Hóngméng was not blessed with either looks or brains, but she had a will of iron and she was shrewd. When tensions between students of different classes began to heat up in our school, she saw her opportunity and started her own separate Red Guard unit made up primarily of "good class" students who were sons and daughters of high-level cadres like herself. Although many students of less desirable backgrounds like myself were both smarter and more talented than she was, she knew her advantage and made sure other Red Guard units such as ours knew it.

"Long live Chairman Máo!" Hóngméng screamed into the microphone. We joined in in unison:

"Long live Chairman Máo!"

"Long live the Revolution!"

"Long live the Revolution!" All around me, people stabbed the air with their Little Red Books in time to the words, hundreds of arms moving as one. Xiǎomèi and I joined the crowd, shouting the words as loudly as we could. A great exhilaration filled me as we chanted. The power of unity and of numbers! The joy of being a part of a great, historical movement!

"Eliminate all ox-ghosts and snake-demons!"

"Smash them, exterminate them!"

"We will not allow capitalist intellectuals to rule our school any longer!"

"Wipe them out, smash them!"

"We will exterminate all of Máo's enemies!" Hóngméng's cry was so passionate that the sound system shrieked in response. She tried again. "We will root out all counter-revolutionary elements in our society!" Again, the speakers let out a long, piercing wail, and a look of deep annoyance crossed her face. Spinning around to face the principal, she lashed out at him with a surprising hatred. "Capitalist pig! Do you admit to your crimes against the People and against the Party?" Another Red Guard pushed the principal roughly from behind. Stumbling two steps forward, he stood with his head bowed and said nothing. His mouth was twitching and his forehead glistened with sweat. "Will you admit to singling out and abusing exemplary revolutionary students while you were principal of Secondary School Number Five? Admit your crimes against the people or we will smash you and your stinking intellectual friends!"

"Principal Wang punished her last year because she was caught cheating on an exam," Xiǎomèi said quietly so others around us would not hear. "Because of her father's position they only made her stay after school and clean classrooms which is not so bad considering she was caught cheating."

"But she lost face," I whispered back. Clearly, Hóngméng had never forgotten the incident. Her voice became more and more shrill as she screamed pronouncements at the principal, her face an explosive red.

The gathering of hundreds was eerily quiet as we pressed forward to see what Principal Wang would do. I felt no affinity with Hóngméng or with her band of arrogant Red Guards. Indeed, I had been a star student at the school and the principal had never treated me badly, yet in those moments I experienced something of an epiphany and an age-old blindfold, as old as Chinese culture itself, finally fell from my eyes. All my life, I had been an obedient daughter, an obedient student, and an obedient citizen because I was afraid of being censured. Unlike Hóngméng, I had never been foolish enough to do anything that brought shame upon myself or my family, but it hit me that day that it was exactly this passivity and fear that had brought China to its knees before the imperialistic Europeans, Americans and Japanese. We had been taught to never question the chains of tradition that bound us so tightly that we could not adapt in a modernized and changing world. The

Communist Party's victory over the feudal Nationalists ushered in a new era, and it was time for us to cast off, violently if necessary, the chains that had bound us for countless centuries.

The realization filled me with a deep hatred for the principal who in that moment represented all the feudal figures in my life who had made me submit to them. Who was this man who had lorded his power over us for so many years? What had he done for us except oppress us? Why did we follow meaningless rules just for the sake of tradition? Chinese people had been blind and passive for far too long. The old order that the principal represented would come crashing down under its own cumbersome weight, and we were thrilled to be the instruments of its demise!

Very subtly, as we watched, the principal's shoulders dropped just a millimeter and it was as if we had won a huge victory. The nervous hush evaporated as we launched into a frenzy of condemnation: "Down with counterrevolutionaries! Down with the stinking intellectual Wang! Down with all stinking intellectuals!" As the fury of the masses swept over me, I lost my mind. Until one actually experiences the magnificent force of the People, one cannot truly appreciate its greatness. Our righteous indignation was as wild and unstoppable as the mighty Yellow River when it breaks through its dams and floods the plains of China with its muddy rage. Xiǎomèi and I were small, insignificant droplets swept along by the deluge, but at least we were there and a part of it all! We shouted the phrases over and over until there was nothing but anger. Sweat ran into our eyes and spit formed at the corners of our mouths as the strength of the revolutionary current propelled us forward.

After some time, Hóngméng held up one hand for silence while her other hand toyed with the heavy copper buckle on the belt that encircled her slender waist. The crowd's roar faded gradually, like a storm tide receding back into the ocean. "Principal Wang," she said in a clear, strong voice as if she were the principal's equal. "I ask you again. Will you confess and repent your reactionary crimes?"

Wang kept his head bowed and did not answer. Hóngméng abruptly spat in his face. In the moment of shock before we or the principal had a chance to react, she unbuckled her belt and dealt a sharp blow to the principal's face with the heavy copper buckle. Wang's head snapped back as he stumbled against the director of administration behind him, but the director's hands were also bound and he could do nothing to help. The principal toppled awkwardly to the ground. Sweat streamed from his forehead as blood flowed from gaps in his mouth where two of his front teeth had been.

"Enemy of the people! Stinking intellectual!" Hóngméng screamed, the belt dangling from her hand. Then, as if possessed by a demon, she whipped the principal over and over again, punctuating the blows with revolutionary slogans. Each time the belt hit Principal Wang, we leaned forward so we could see better. Red Guards from Hóngméng's group drew in like a pack of rabid dogs. They took turns whipping and kicking the prostrate form long after it was clear that the man had lost consciousness.

When the students finished with the principal, they turned to Shīfu who had been standing quietly on the stage all this time. I could not help but notice, even in my excitement, that his composure set him apart from the others. He had averted his face to avoid seeing the vicious beating, but his face was calm. People around me strained forward to see who we would be struggling against next. The humid summer air reeked of sour sweat, yet Shīfu stood like a tall bamboo in the middle of a winter storm: strong, lithe, composed.

I would have expected nothing less from someone of his stature and character, but to witness his presence in such a mad situation affected me deeply, and my body began to tremble so violently that I would have buckled had it not been for Xiǎomèi's steadying hand on my arm. Her look reminded me that I was a soldier on a critical mission. Good soldiers do not allow anything—especially sentimentality—to weaken their resolve. I was only a small droplet working for the betterment of society. Taking a deep breath, I stood up taller in my uniform and willed my body to be strong.

A Red Guard from our unit, an attractive boy with a square jaw and straight nose, stepped forward to the microphone and waited patiently for the crowd to hush. "Today is a day of victory for the Revolution, my comrades!" He spoke well, his voice confident and strong. Despite my resolve, I began to sweat profusely and could not stop shaking even in the intense summer heat. "Today, not only are we smashing the stinking intellectuals and rotten capitalists in our school, but we are also making a clean sweep with the superstitious past! Even while we have been working hard to destroy the Four Olds within our society, our industrious working group has uncovered subversive forces in our own community that have been eating away at our progress. We must root out all reactionary enemies among us! We must do away with ignorance and superstition once and for all!"

"Smash the Four Olds! Smash all reactionary enemies!" we chanted.

"Here before you stands one of the last pillars of the feudal past. Today, we are toppling all pillars of superstition! We are freeing ourselves from reactionary thinking! Long live the Revolution!" Several students pushed Shīfu forward.

"In a most exemplary self-criticism submitted just this week, ninth grader Comrade Zhū Zhìxīn of class twenty-six came forward to reveal a most odious charlatan in our society." He paused to allow the crowd to quiet down. "For years, Zhū Zhìxīn was forced to live with one of the most evil and insidious of counter-revolutionaries in China. This 'Mongol healer', this charlatan, has been hiding in our midst, but Zhū Zhìxīn's strong revolutionary heart prevailed, and he has uncovered the evil practices of the so-called qigong master Zhū Shǒuliàng! Zhū Shǒuliàng has tricked many people into thinking that he can perform miracles of healing. These are false and dangerous claims! This snake preys on the weak in our society the way wild dogs prey on babies!"

The crowd became especially attentive at the mention of Shīfu's name. He was a well-known and well-respected figure in our community even among those who did not practice qigong, and a questioning murmur began to bubble up within the audience. Sensing their doubt, my classmate smiled and scanned the crowd until our eyes met. He saluted me as I mounted the stage. I planted my feet wide apart in the center of the stage, drew a deep breath, and spoke into the microphone.

"We all know that our beloved Chairman and the Party take care of us in every way whether we are healthy or sick. Our beloved Chairman has assured us that we can extinguish the four pests and cure the diseases of China using the practices of modern medicine. And what is modern medicine based on? It is based on modern science and technology!"

"Yes, science and technology. Science and technology are the basis of modern medicine!" the crowd murmured.

"As our beloved Chairman himself has said, people who promote qigong are no better than circus entertainers, snake oil salesmen, and street hawkers. Zhū Shǒuliàng claims to be a practitioner of traditional Chinese medicine, but what is the scientific basis of his so-called healing? What medicines does he use? His 'medicine' is made up of lies! He is a swindler and a cheat! Anyone who claims he can cure people of diseases without proper medical training is lying and is an enemy of the People. This man is a dangerous threat to the Revolution!" As nervous as I was, I spoke with the conviction that comes from speaking the truth, and as I heard my own, strong voice ring out over the field, amplified by dozens of loudspeakers, my body stopped shaking.

Their attention harnessed, the crowd responded with a roar of assent: Zhū Shǒuliàng was a swindler! His swindling days were over! Zhū Shǒuliàng deserved to be punished for cheating so many innocent proletariat!

Members of my unit shoved Shīfu to his knees and forced him

to bow his head even lower while another classmate stepped up to the microphone and threw a question out to the crowd: "Can old dogs fly?" We responded with jeers and cold laughter. "Why don't you show us how you can soar, you old counterrevolutionary dog!" Several Red Guards surrounded Shīfu and bent him forward into the jet plane pose, jerking his bound hands up behind him. Shīfu leaned forward at the waist, but the student soldiers were careless. They yanked his hands upwards until his shoulders gave with a sudden pop, one after the other. Grimacing with pain, his face wet with tears and sweat, Shīfu did not appear to hear the insults we hurled at him as the crowd went wild. Having tasted blood, we wanted more.

My comrades got the idea to force Shīfu to sing the "Ox-Ghosts and Snake Demons" song. He remained silent even when they slapped his face and shoved the microphone tauntingly in front of his mouth, but we all knew the simple tune and lyrics by heart.

*I am an ox-ghost and snake-demon*
*I am an ox-ghost and snake-demon*
*I am guilty, I am guilty*
*I have committed crimes against the people*
*So the people are my dictator*
*I must lower my head and admit my guilt*
*I must be obedient*
*I am not allowed to speak or act without permission*
*If I speak or act without permission*
*You will smash me to pieces*
*You will smash me to pieces!*

Hóngméng had been standing to the side but stepped forward now, belt in hand. With a well-practiced whipping motion that came from the elbow, she lashed Shīfu across the forehead. It was only after a few moments that a small rivulet of crimson formed across his brow. The second blow landed squarely on the back of his head at the base of the skull. The crowd pressed forward, suddenly silent.

The master's form remained kneeling for the span of a single breath. Then slowly, slowly, with the ponderous weight of a gigantic bamboo, he crumpled forward onto his face, his hands still bound tightly behind him.

My fellow Red Guards led Shīfu's son, the stunned young Zhū Zhìxīn, onto the stage pumping his right arm victoriously: he was a revolutionary hero for standing up to his reactionary father, and his formidable opponent lay dying at his feet.

"May Chairman Máo live for ten thousand years, ten million years!" We cried again and again, our voices hoarse.

# Arrival



NATALIE EMERGED WEAK AND pale from the cocoon of her sleeping bag where she had spent the past week. She was tired of being sick and laid up in the hostel, and she had learned her lesson to not walk around Beijing for hours without a face mask on a day when the API shot past 380. How could she have known that being exposed to that level of air pollution would incapacitate her for a week? With her ultra-healthy, yoga-driven lifestyle, Natalie was rarely ill which was why the high fever, body aches and deep cough had been a surprise. Now, to make up for time lost, she needed to redouble her efforts in her search for housing and a studio space for her yoga business, but the prospect of venturing out into the huge, sprawling city again was daunting.

Natalie showered and put on her favorite dress—a white, one-shouldered number splashed with huge bird of paradise blooms—pulled on black, knee-high boots, and attempted to tame her unruly, orange-dyed mane with a clip studded with crystals. She frowned at her image in the mirror—oval face, even features, nose that was broader than she liked, bony frame, well-muscled shoulders and arms from the yoga—and reached for plum-colored lipstick and mascara. She did not usually wear make-up, but today she needed a little help going out into the world. She had badly misjudged how long it would take her to get situated in Beijing and needed to regroup, but it was too late in the day to make any progress on that front. A flyer next to the hostel's front desk advertised live music by

Inner Mongolian musicians at a café just down the street. It was just the thing to take her mind off things if only for a couple of hours.

Sandglass Café was a drab storefront by day but transformed into a cozy watering hole that was frequented by ex-pats at night. Incandescent bulbs suspended within red, blown-glass globes cast a warm light over the antique, wood-lattice door panels that lined the walls, simple and rough-cut wooden tables and chairs, and an assortment of plush armchairs and well-worn leather wingback chairs near the back where the musicians were setting up. Natalie settled onto a red, overstuffed, velveteen loveseat across from the musicians and set her mug of tea on the low table in front of her.

She watched the three musicians tune the two-stringed horse head fiddles they held between their knees and wondered if she would stay long enough in China to visit Inner Mongolia. As the musicians bowed little snatches of song that sounded like horses neighing and birds chirping, she envisioned lush green grassland that stretched as far as the eye could see: a landscape free of people. As a Bay Area native, Natalie was no stranger to big city living, but after only a month of navigating the crushing crowds, cacophony, and smog-choked streets of Beijing, she longed for the expansiveness of wind-swept bluffs overlooking the ocean or the hush of the redwood forests back home. She never needed to drive more than an hour before she could lose herself completely in Nature. Had it been a huge mistake for her to quit her yoga teaching jobs and sell off the scant furniture she owned? She was not sure which she missed more in Beijing: Nature or human companionship, neither of which she had been able to find.

The café was quickly filling with foreigners casually holding frosty Heineken bottles and a smattering of locals sipping Tsingdao beer on the warm summer evening. It was not long before the small space was clamoring with multiple languages and Friday night laughter. Natalie was glad she was not among the boisterous young Americans and Brits who spoke too loudly and with the self-assurance of ex-pats who were cool enough to be living abroad yet who assiduously sought the company of people just like themselves. She was so absorbed in watching the other ex-pats that she did not at first notice that a thirty-some year-old Chinese man wearing a dark red dress shirt and black trousers had come up to where she was sitting. When she finally looked up, he smiled but made no effort to hide the fact that he had been looking at her.

"Is anyone sitting here?" he asked her in Mandarin. His accent was impeccable and polished, well-educated. It was only then that Natalie realized that all the seats had been taken, most of the other patrons were standing, and she was taking up the whole loveseat. She hurried to make room for him.

As soon as the man sat down, Natalie felt the electricity of an immediate and unmistakable attraction. He was not handsome per se, but he had strong, southern Chinese features that were not unattractive: sleepy eyes beneath thick black brows suggested he held his cards close to his chest but smile wrinkles around his eyes made him seem approachable. His lips were full for a man, and Natalie thought about her mother's claim that men with thicker lips were known to be faithful. This observation had come after she had divorced Natalie's average-lipped father.

Natalie glanced at the man a second and then, surreptitiously, a third time. He looked like a man who knew his mind and went after what he wanted in life. He had come to the café alone, unusual for a Chinese, and unlike the other patrons who were nursing their beers or mixed drinks, he was also drinking tea. She debated whether she should start a conversation but did not know how to begin so was relieved when he took a slow sip, carefully placed his mug on the table, then looked over at her. "I may be mistaken," he said, still in Chinese, "but you don't look like a native."

Natalie almost laughed out loud. Chinese features notwithstanding, it was obvious she was not a local. As modern as the city had seemed at first glance with its tall, glittering buildings, she found Beijingers to be politically and culturally more conservative than people she had met in Shanghai or Hong Kong. She had never been made to feel so self-conscious about the little nose stud, the multiple ear-piercings, or the dyed hair. With her tight, strappy yoga tops and the flashy rings that adorned most of her fingers, Natalie was as conspicuously out of place in Beijing as a parrot she had spotted in a tree on her way in from the airport. She had turned around to stare at the scarlet and blue escapee, a bright spot of color against the drab landscape, until it had faded from view. How would it survive in the city or weather the upcoming winter?

"My hometown is San Francisco," she said, knowing full well that the Chinese term she used, *jiāxiāng,* usually refers to a place in China where one's family is from.

"Ah, a Chinese American," he said as if that explained everything. He sounded amused. "I'm not from here either. I've lived here for twenty years but I'm still an outsider. Beijing is not an easy place to break into." When his gaze lingered on her for just a fraction of a second too long, Natalie willed herself to stop fidgeting with the six rings she wore on her left hand, turning them around and around on her fingers. It was only after all the stones were facing up again that she looked up. "Are you a student?" he asked.

"Oh, I graduated a few years ago. I'm a yoga teacher."

"Yoga," he said slowly. "I confess I don't know much about yoga, but it seems to have more potential than most of the trends that come and go so quickly these days. If I'm remembering correctly, yoga is from India where they have been practicing for thousands of years. Anything that has lasted that long must have some value. In China we have qigong, *tàijíquán, gōngfu,* but we've had a rough history. We've lost a lot of our heritage. Plus, no one is interested in that stuff anymore except old people. But yoga. Yoga is hip. It has foreign appeal. Everyone in America is practicing yoga. Am I right?" He grinned. There it was again, that frank, easy, eye contact.

"You seem to know a little about it. Do you practice?"

"Oh, a few classes here and there. I'm really out of shape," he said, though to her yoga instructor eyes he looked as though he regularly spent time in a gym.

"All the more reason to practice."

"Maybe you can teach me," he said with that glimmer of amusement.

Before Natalie could respond, the horse head fiddle ensemble launched into their first piece. The fast, syncopated melody in a pentatonic scale sounded just like horses galloping, transporting Natalie to the vast, wind-swept steppes of a much different time. Thousands of horses thundered across the grasslands as Chinggis Khan's hordes subjugated the entire Eurasian continent with their superior archery skills and willingness to raze entire cities. Their battle flags whipped into blurs of color by the relentless Central Asian wind, the Mongolian warriors terrorized, subjugated and killed millions in their path. What would it have been like to live as either ruthless soldier or plundered townsfolk? Natalie spun the rings on her fingers around and around as she listened.

Just before the stampeding horses lost complete control, the song stepped seamlessly into a minor key and slowed to a long, mournful ode to the grassland, the mother of all. Grazing herds moved leisurely across verdant steppes. Horses neighed into the wailing wind. The nomad's peace was married to a deep melancholy. Birth and death, abundance and lack, everything was balanced precariously between the deep blue sky and the ever-giving earth. Then, charged with the enthusiasm of only half-tamed horses at play, the piece ended with another rousing gallop across the grasslands.

"Powerful," the man murmured as the café rang with applause. "Mongolians have retained something primal that the *Hànzú*, Han Chinese, lost long ago. That bestseller *Wolf Totem* speaks to something we Han people have lost."

The music had drawn them into an easy camaraderie, an immediate intimacy. Natalie wondered at his use of the term "we": was she with her American flamboyance included in that greater Chinese whole? As different as she was from this stranger, was there a common thread that brought them together after all? Back in the States, Natalie had never felt that she belonged anywhere—not at school, not within the predominantly white yoga community, certainly not in her mother's conservative, immigrant Chinese church. Now that she was here, she was acutely aware of her status as an outsider even as she yearned for connection.

They did not speak for the rest of the performance, but when the last piece ended and the musicians put their instruments down amidst enthusiastic applause and whistles, Natalie sighed. "I wonder what it would be like to live in Inner Mongolia," she said and was suddenly aware that she had shared something very personal with the man, more personal than the words alone indicated. She thought about how fleeting human connections were: a few words exchanged with a stranger in a café before they each went their way.

Natalie expected the man to get up and leave now that the performance was over, but he leaned back and crossed his left ankle over his right knee. He stretched leisurely then interlaced his fingers behind his head. "Why don't you go check it out?" he asked. She could not decide if his expression was sleepy, amused, or good-naturedly sly.

"I need to get settled first. I don't even have a place to live yet," Natalie replied. She thought about the dozens of rental units she had seen that had been within her budget, but they were uniformly disappointing. There were dreary utilitarian dives circa 1980s communist China with their dingy tile floors and walls painted halfway up in turquoise blue. On the other end of the spectrum, there were the nouveau riche rococo apartments of the newly prosperous middle class: dark laminate wood flooring and over-sized, fake leather couch sets were illuminated by flickering karaoke lighting that middle-aged landlords proudly switched on and off for effect. Either way, the polluted sunlight oozing through plastic curtains did little to lighten up the post-Communist gloom. Nothing felt like home.

The man was quiet for a moment. "I know we have only just met, but since you mention it, I've been looking for a roommate for my spare bedroom. Someone to look after the place when I'm not around. I'm not home much since my work takes me to Shanghai most of the time so it might work well for someone like you."

Natalie studied the stranger's face. He looked back at her with a small smile, his eyebrows slightly raised. There was an openness and sincerity about him. She trusted him for some reason. "That's very generous of you," she said, "but I don't even know your name."

"You can call me Malcolm," he said with a wink, his name being the first thing he had said to her in English.

"I'm *Nàtǎlì*," she said, giving him her Chinese name. "Do you mind my asking what you do?"

Malcolm chuckled as if she had made a small joke. "Oh, this and that. I'm an entrepreneur. Export mainly. It's a job," he said with a shrug. "What about you? Do you plan to teach yoga?"

"I want to start my own yoga business here. I think there is a market for it, and China is the place to be right now for new enterprises. It'd be much easier to start a business here than in the States."

"That seems like an accurate assessment. What kind of business do you have in mind?" He seemed genuinely interested, and before she knew it, she was sharing the dream she had been carefully nurturing for more than two years.

"A yoga business is simple to start and run. I just need a studio space with a good wooden floor, and the rest I can handle myself," she said, gaining traction as she went. "There's not much overhead and there won't be any inventory to worry about because I won't sell any products while the business is still getting established. I can handle the scheduling, bookings, marketing and advertising—I studied graphic design in college."

"It's a lot for one person," Malcolm observed, but he was listening closely.

"Before I came here, I was teaching twenty-five classes a week at three different studios. I was also interning at a major marketing firm in downtown San Francisco. I can do even more if I'm working for myself." It felt good to finally be talking to someone.

"I can vouch for that—nothing beats being your own boss. But even if the business you're thinking of is relatively simple, starting any new venture in China requires the right connections. You'll need a Chinese partner who knows the ropes who'd be willing to underwrite your business. But I'm sure you know that already."

Natalie realized with a jolt that she had not known. For months she had dreamed about the autonomy and freedom she would have when she opened her own studio, but it had never occurred to her that she would need a Chinese business partner. What else had she not considered in her naïveté?

Natalie's mother would be the first to point out that she was too impulsive and that she always acted before thinking things through. *You will never make it in Beijing*, her mother had told her. *What do you know about running your own business? We don't have any family or connections left in Beijing—my family was lucky to get out before the Communists took over. You would be all alone.*

Natalie had disagreed. Things were different this time. Her move to Beijing was not a rash spur of the moment decision; she had spent months planning and researching the possibilities. She had a business plan and had consulted with her father's business associates. They had been indulgent and avuncular when she asked them about starting her own business, but she realized now that they had nothing at stake. Moreover, all of her father's friends were based in Taiwan. Even if they had contacts in China and were willing to help, time was not on her side. She had already lost a week because of the illness, and she had nothing to show for the month she had been in country. The cherished vision of her own, cozy little yoga studio flickered and moved just beyond reach, but she would hate to prove her mother right.

Malcolm saw her look of panic. "You know," he said, "it just so happens that I've been looking to expand and do something different. From what I've seen, yoga is more than a passing fad in China. I think it has enormous business potential. I can take a look at your business plan if you have one."

"That would be very kind of you," she replied, still trying to absorb the enormity of her oversight and fighting to banish her mother's told-you-so voice from her mind. "But I should mention that my goal in teaching yoga is not strictly to make money. For me, yoga is a lifestyle and a philosophy. It can benefit a lot of people as a discipline."

Malcolm's only response was a broad grin. As they studied each other in the long pause that followed, Natalie knew that he found her idealism naïve. After spending only a couple of hours in his company, Natalie could already see that while Malcolm was friendly, the friendliness masked some depth and private thoughts. Those sleepy eyes gave away little.

"Tell you what," he said. "If your idea is worth backing, I'll consider being your business partner." Seeing her look, he leaned back on the loveseat and interlaced his fingers behind his head again. Gazing thoughtfully at the red globes suspended high above the table in front of them, he continued, "Everything has to check out, of course, but I felt something of an intuitive hunch when I saw you, and I always follow my instincts when it comes to business matters. The business I started ten years ago now operates in Beijing, Shanghai and Chengdu. I know people. And," he said with a broad smile she already recognized, "I'm willing to support a good cause." He turned back to see how she was taking the new information. Then he said it just as she was thinking it, but his tone was ultra-casual, offhand almost. "Believe me, I never propose something as important as this to just anyone I meet. But this feels right. Call it fate I guess."

"I'd like to see your place," Natalie said, also keeping her tone casual although what she really wanted to do was jump up and do a happy dance.

"I don't have any plans for the rest of the evening," he replied.

The musicians had already packed up and were swapping stories with the bartender, frosty beer bottles in hand, when Natalie and Malcolm left the café, stepping out into the brightly lit Beijing night together.

*"I'm sorry to bother you," the young woman says again. "You don't know me, but I didn't know where else to go." She looks stricken. Wú nods, listening, as she fills the kettle with water for tea.*

*"I can still welcome you even if I don't know you," Wú says. "Have you eaten?" The young woman hesitates then shakes her head. Wú brings out a plate of sesame-covered shāobǐng and cuts a few of the flaky pastries in half to reveal the sweet red bean and black sesame paste fillings. "I made these this morning," she says and smiles when the young woman's face lights up. She really is too thin, like an angular, young fledgling who has not grown out her flight feathers yet.*

*"You are so kind," the young woman says. "I wish I had met you when I came here two years ago."*

*"How would things have been different if we had met two years ago?" Wú asks her.*

# Transplants

INNER MONGOLIA, 1968

I AWOKE WITH A start in the early hours of the morning still exhausted but with a sense that something was wrong. Struggling to break free of the wooliness of sleep, the realization came to me slowly: the fire had died out. Without a fire burning in our *ménggǔbāo* or *ger*, as the local Mongolians called the felt tent that provided scant protection from the elements, we would quickly freeze to death in the minus forty-degree temperatures. I struck a match and glanced around the cramped circular space: Xiǎomèi and the other girl from Beijing were wrapped tightly in their thick quilts. All that could be seen of them were long strands of hair that trailed across their pillows like fugitives. I sighed. It had been Xiǎomèi's turn to keep the fire burning that night, but of the three of us she had the most delicate constitution despite her unwavering enthusiasm. The day's hard work in the deep snow had completely worn her out, and no one could blame her for falling dead asleep. If I had not woken up, however, none of us would have gotten up in the morning.

I took a deep breath. Teeth clenched hard, I threw back the heavy blankets, flung a sheepskin-lined *deel* around my hunched shoulders and yanked on padded trousers and wool felt boots. Though I moved quickly, the *deel* felt like a blanket of ice around me, and I was shivering so hard I could hardly breathe. Dropping into a squat in front of the stove, I placed some dried dung on the few orange embers that glowed weakly in the stove's belly. My breath came out white in the darkness as I blew gently on the coals. Instead of igniting, however, the dung began to smoke profusely. Coughing and squinting, I slammed the stove door shut. Even after a month of living in the countryside, I was still not used to the acridness of dung smoke.

Still coughing, I stumbled over to the door and just avoided hitting my forehead on the low doorframe as I flung the door open. Smoke billowed out into the night while a sweeping vista, bare and impassive, greeted me. The bleakness of the Inner Mongolian landscape never failed to unsettle me. The sun had not yet risen and the moon had already set, but the snow-covered ground glowed a pale blue in the darkness, and the sky was punctuated with thousands upon thousands of stars. Everything was so exposed here. A person could easily get lost in the vastness of the frontier, and I ached for the protective walls of the city that was my home.

On the first night the three of us stayed in the *ger*, a strange, desolate chorus rose up around us that made my scalp prickle. It was only after a moment that I realized what the eerie singing meant: wolves. In the distance, the village dogs went wild. Chains clanked as they lunged against their tethers half-howling half-barking mournful challenges. Exhausted from the long journey from Beijing, we sat on our beds and stared wordlessly at each other in the flickering candlelight. This was our site of reeducation. Living and working among the peasants had sounded so romantic and revolutionary when we were still in Beijing, but after we arrived in Inner Mongolia we saw the reality of our situation and realized how difficult our lives would be. What could we possibly learn from such a savage place?

The fire. There was no time to shrink before the Mongolian sky or to dwell on our deep disappointment. My fingers, toes and nose were already numb, and tears produced by the smoke were already frozen on my eyelashes. Shivering so hard I could barely think, I cast around for something that would get the fire going again. We had run out of kindling and paper was precious. The candle in the middle of the table. Keenly aware of the locals' certain disapproval of such wastefulness but feeling desperate, I dripped some candle wax onto the embers. After several long minutes, the small pool of wax ignited and began to burn before the dung, grudgingly, began to burn a little as well. I hardly breathed as I nurtured the small flame.

When the fire was burning strongly again, I sat back on my heels with a sigh. Before I knew it, I was wiping away tears with the sleeves of my *deel*: deep relief that we had fire and would soon be warm again. The mortifying realization a heartbeat later: I, a Red Guard who had been on the verge of graduating from secondary school with honors before the Cultural Revolution began, was reduced to this.

Many struggle sessions followed the one in which my testimony against Shīfu led to his death. Not all the sessions were as violent, but scores of intellectuals and people accused of being counterrevolutionary died, committed suicide or were left permanently scarred in the early years of the Cultural Revolution. The first few deaths were difficult to witness, but as a soldier of the revolution, I reminded myself of the Chairman's words: violence was justified when dealing with our enemies.

Our work kept us so busy that the question of whether people were rightly or wrongly accused did not cross my mind. I even began to resent those we targeted for being backwards and causing us so much trouble. If I had any misgivings about the rightness of our actions, all doubts were completely washed away by the exhilaration that filled us when Xiǎoměi and I went to Tiān'ānmén Square to pay our respects to Chairman Máo. No words can describe the experience of seeing our great leader in person and knowing that we had his blessing. It was like being in the presence of a god. Though we could only see him from afar, we were surrounded by hundreds of thousands of like-minded soldiers who were unified in the work of ushering in a New China that would finally bring economic prosperity, social reforms, equality for women, and much, much more.

After the Tiān'ānmén rallies, Xiǎomèi and I returned home buzzing with an ironclad commitment to the work. When Chairman Máo urged us to engage in revolutionary exchange with our brothers and sisters in the countryside for the Great Link-Up, of course we went. Our red armbands served as passes for free train fare, food, and lodging as we traveled deep into the countryside and visited the most sacred revolutionary sites: the magnificent Jǐnggāng Mountains where the Red Army was born, Yán'ān, the birthplace of the Communist revolution and, of course, Sháoshān, Máo's birthplace.

Both Xiǎomèi and I were born and raised in Beijing so it was the first time we traveled outside the city to see the places we had heard so much about since our earliest school days. We finally saw with our own eyes how vast and great our country was. Though we had spent countless hours back in Beijing discussing the situation of the peasantry in our study sessions of the Chairman's Thought, it was during the Great Link-Up that we saw how our countrymen actually lived, and our hearts went out to the hardy and long-suffering people whose futures we were working to improve. Wherever we went, the peasants welcomed and fed us. We, in turn, conducted struggle sessions, led study groups, and handed out copies of *Quotations from Chairman Máo* and *Selected Works of Máo Zédōng*. Though many of the peasants could not read, they received the books with great gratitude, holding the little red volumes reverently to their chests with both hands.

Hundreds of thousands of Red Guards traveled around the country at that time, and over the course of those glorious few months, we met students from all over China. It was a marvelous time in which we compared stories about our revolutionary activities and made many friends as we spread the fiery winds of the Revolution to even the remotest corners of our great country.

In 1968, in the second year of the Cultural Revolution, Chairman Máo told us that it was our duty to go "up to the mountains and down to the countryside" so we could be reeducated by the peasantry. We were to live and work among them, serve them, and learn from them. Together, we would build a new socialist countryside. Though the idea of leaving the city was daunting, Xiǎomèi and I never questioned our duty to go even when it meant that our city residence statuses would be revoked and transferred to our sites of reeducation. I could have applied to stay on in Beijing to take care of my elderly grandmother, my only living relative at the time since my father had died in the hard labor camp, but I ignored her pleas to stay because, simply put, I lived for a higher purpose. Everything was secondary to my sense of duty to our country—it was the only thing I had known since I could walk and talk: love for our great Chairman and loyalty to the Party. Xiǎomèi volunteered to go to the countryside because she was just as committed as I was, but much to her family's consternation, she did not have a choice because all of her class was deemed a "Red Class" which meant they were all dispatched to the countryside.

When we learned that we had been assigned to the Inner Mongolian Autonomous Region, I received the news with mixed feelings. Inner Mongolia was where my father had been sent to be reformed through hard labor, and it was where he died a few months after I burned all his books. He did not survive the first winter there, and when word came that he had died without being rehabilitated, my grandmother was almost split apart with the grief of mourning her only son.

I, however, did not shed any tears on my father's behalf. I loved him, but he represented everything we were working to destroy. Even my earliest memories of him—always at his desk, studying his foreign literature or writing lesson plans—confirmed that his life had been overtaken by a slavish devotion to the feudal West. His work took precedence over everything, and the only times he engaged with me were when he taught me about Western Romanticism. His status as a scholar was everything to him, and without it, he was nothing. I regretted that he did not live to see the New China that we were building but accepted that he, like many others, was a necessary casualty of the revolution.

The fact that I was being sent to where he had failed lent my assignment even more gravity, and I felt a deep sense of responsibility. While our small town was a distance away from his site of rehabilitation, it seemed particularly meaningful that I was being sent there not to be reformed but to keep the revolutionary fires stoked in one of the remotest corners of our country. Only later did I understand that the frontier was where people were sent to be forgotten so my fate was supposed to be the same as my father's despite all the ways I had demonstrated my loyalty. But at the time, acute awareness of my father's failure made me eager to prove that I was stronger, more enlightened, and worthy.

We knew very little about our reeducation site, but we had heard that Mongolians were a noble and hardy people known for their beautiful folk music. We imagined ourselves working alongside the herdsmen on the beautiful green grassland and learning to sing their pastoral songs. The reality of our relocation was very different, of course. We had not anticipated the locals' cool reception when we arrived in the small township of about two thousand inhabitants that was deep, deep in the countryside. It would be my home for the next twelve years. We knew nothing about the cultural and political tensions between the local Mongolians and the ever-increasing number of Han Chinese settlers which included *zhīqīng* youth like ourselves, and we did not know about the rising tide of Mongolian nationalism that was a response to the Party's attempts to assimilate ethnic Mongolians into the greater Chinese whole.


Wide awake now, I pulled up a low stool to sit by the stove as the fire gradually warmed the little *ger*. The other girls were still fast asleep, but I could not sleep thinking about the official meeting that would take place that evening in the school gymnasium. It would be our first real opportunity to meet and learn from the herdsmen we had come to work with, and I was both excited and apprehensive. That first uneven month of getting settled and adjusting to the harsh life of the countryside had left little room for planning, and I looked forward to finally embarking on the work we had come to do. After staring into the flames for some time, I retrieved a notebook and pencil and began to make notes for myself and the other students so we would be prepared when we spoke with the locals.

There were five of us assigned to the township: three girls and two boys, all from Beijing, ranging from seventeen-year-old Xiǎomèi to a boy we called Poet, a twenty-one-year-old student whose thick glasses made his eyes look huge. The son of teachers, like myself, he alone in our group had the distinction of having attended one year of university before the Cultural Revolution suspended all regular education. I noticed right away that he, like Xiǎomèi, was more thoughtful than the other two students. Quiet and shy by nature, Poet was more of an observer than a leader. He spoke sparingly but quickly demonstrated that he was a good judge of both situations and character. It was not long before the rest of the students and I found ourselves often turning to him for advice. While I was the most outspoken and therefore the de facto leader of the group, Poet was the one who buoyed our spirits with his quiet wisdom and good sense when we felt discouraged.

Before we left Beijing, we were told that our job as part of a newly formed production and construction team was to help the herders in the area increase their productivity by at least twofold within four years. The area was abundant in natural resources, full of untapped potential, but it was lagging in production. Many of the herders had yet to see the grand proletarian vision of the future where the employment of modern methods in animal husbandry could greatly increase production. Our township needed to do its part in the collective building of a strong nation.

I spent a long time that night sketching out a plan for how we would help the herders achieve the production goals. Finally, just as the faint blue glow of dawn began to light up the glass panes at the top of the *ger*, I put more dung on the fire and tucked the notebook under my mattress. I looked forward to consulting Xiǎomèi and Poet about my ideas after I had slept a couple of hours.

We were so busy repairing and building new communal livestock pens and runs that the day passed quickly. Though exhausted by the end of the day, as we often were that first winter, Xiǎomèi, Poet, the other students, and I were in good spirits as we headed to the school for the evening meeting. I was wearing my Red Guard uniform which never failed to remind me of the camaraderie and solidarity we enjoyed as dedicated soldiers of the revolution. Xiǎomèi, also wearing her uniform, looked smart and resolute.

I felt great pride when, upon entering the gymnasium, I saw the brilliant vermillion and yellow of our country's flag next to the two tables in the front where we would sit with the local officials. The cavernous room rang with our footsteps as we strode past the rows of chairs to take our seats. When I saluted the Brigade Leader, a Mongolian woman by the name of Dorj, she did not smile nor did she salute me back. The other two officials nodded in our direction but continued to converse only with each other in Mongolian. They had welcomed us at the train station when we arrived but, to our puzzlement, we had not had an opportunity to speak with them about our mission over the course of the month nor had they reached out to us. I resolved then and there to learn Mongolian if it would help us accomplish our mission.

Very few people were in the gymnasium when we arrived which was not surprising because we were, as was our habit, early. However, as the meeting start time came and went and most of the seats remained empty, I started exchanging questioning looks with Xiǎomèi and Poet. At half past the hour when the local officials still made no effort to engage with us or to start the meeting, I leaned towards the microphone on the table in front of me.

"Welcome, comrades," I said, glancing around at the two dozen or so ruddy, unsmiling faces in front of us. The herders, all men, were dressed in traditional sheepskin-lined *deel* with orange and yellow sashes and black boots. Some of them wore wide-brimmed hats while others wore fur-lined caps. "Long live Chairman Máo and long live the revolution! We are gathered here this evening to talk about how your—how our—township will join the great work that is happening all around the country to realize the great proletarian vision of the future! We come from the city to humbly learn from and work alongside you so that together we can increase yields and do our part to build a bright and strong Communist country in which we all enjoy peace and prosperity."

To my complete bewilderment, few of the herders looked up or even acknowledged that they heard me. Xiǎomèi and I, along with our fellow Red Guards, had led meetings for hundreds if not thousands of people all over the country, and this was not how our countrymen usually responded when we spoke. Completely unsettled and more than a little confused, I nevertheless soldiered on. I asked many questions about production numbers and how they raised their animals. Xiǎomèi invited them to explain the many factors that affect production, but our queries were largely met with an intractable silence. Throughout all of this, none of the officials spoke up or offered to help though they were observing both us and the herders carefully.

The rest of the meeting limped along until we did not have

anything more to ask or say so adjourned half an hour early. As disappointed as I was, I knew that we just needed to find a different approach in the same way that water always finds the path of least resistance. One Mongolian man in the back of the room seemed to embody the group's collective resistance towards both our presence as well as the mission we outlined for them. While he was quite young, others had turned to him for guidance although his only contributions were terse, reluctant responses in a heavily accented Mandarin. Like the other herders, he was dressed in a worn and stained blue *deel* with a faded yellow sash. Broad-shouldered and powerfully built, he sat in the last row with his heavy, black, upturned-toed boots planted wide apart, arms crossed over his chest, and a deep frown on his sun and wind-reddened face. I approached him at the end of the meeting.

"Comrade, we have not met yet. What is your name?"

The man glanced at me, and his look was not friendly. "My name is Bayarbat. People call me Bayaraa," he said finally, reluctantly. He made as if to leave but I was not to be so easily deterred.

"Bayaraa, I see that you are a leader among your peers," I said. "They trust you, and if you would use your influence, we can accomplish our goals together."

"We all do what we can to support the revolution," Bayaraa said, but his tone was flat, and he turned away.

"Long live the revolution," I replied. "We need your help. You are a production team leader. Isn't it your duty to increase production for the good of our country?" Though he had already taken a few steps away, Bayaraa turned around and looked me fully in the face for a long moment sizing me up. He was more than a head taller than I was, twice as wide, and he was frowning. I drew myself up, threw back my shoulders and looked right back at him, my Red Guard uniform giving me courage. I knew that if we were to succeed, we needed this man's cooperation. After many long moments of silence in which neither of us looked away, he spoke.

"We can double our herds and increase production. We can even reach the targeted numbers." I started to smile, but he was not finished speaking. "But it would be extremely foolish to do so. There is a balance in Nature that must be respected. If we graze too many animals, the grassland will die. If the grassland dies, there will be no more animals. If there are no more animals, there will be no more production and we will all be eating sand. You are from the city. You do not understand life here. You have never cared for livestock, nor have you lived as we do. All you know are numbers on a piece of paper." With that, Bayaraa turned his back on me and walked out.

# Meeting the Master



"I WILL NEVER BE a dancer now, but if it were not for Master Zhu I would not even be able to walk. After the car accident, my parents took me to see all kinds of doctors, but only Master Zhu could cure me." Natalie just caught Dāndān's words, flung over her shoulder, before the young woman leaned over her handlebars and began to pedal as fast as she could, daring Natalie to keep up. Natalie caught up just in time to hear Dāndān laugh. As they raced each other through Beijing's narrow *hútong* alleyways, she smiled every time she glanced over at her friend. It was Dāndān to a T: leaning into the wind, an enormous grin on her face, pedaling as hard as she could, long hair rippling behind her like a black silk scarf. Dāndān's enthusiasm for virtually everything she encountered was infectious, and Natalie found herself a little in love with her new friend. Her sincere interest in yoga was gratifying especially given the discipline she brought to the practice as a former dancer, but Natalie quickly discovered that the seriousness was confined only to the studio. The minute they left the health club where Natalie taught classes, the impish Dāndān who found joy in everything burst forward. From delighting over the discovery of a novel dessert at a newly opened bakery to exclaiming over the way the gingko leaves filtered the late afternoon sunlight—her hair flowing loose down to her waist as she tilted her head up to gaze into the branches—she was like one of the red lanterns that graced the entryways of the businesses they passed: a bright, cheerful, swaying spot of color against the drab gray of the city.

"I want to know if there are correlations between yoga and qigong," Natalie said, trying to not pant as they continued to race through the *hútong*. "Maybe the qigong master can help me understand this part of Chinese culture the way someone like you understands it."

"Master Zhu is absolutely the person to talk to. He's the preeminent qigong master in all of China and director of the only public qigong institution in Beijing. You're fortunate to have me as a connection," Dāndān informed Natalie with a wink.

Before she came to China, Natalie's cultural heritage had always been a misty abstraction if not a source of awkwardness. She had sometimes made solo forays into San Francisco's Chinatown as a teenager, but she never identified with what she found there. The shopkeepers and waiters spoke Cantonese, for one, and many had lived in the area for several generations whereas Natalie's parents were first generation Mandarin speaking immigrants from China via Taiwan. When she was very young and her parents were still together, they had taken her to watch the yearly Chinese New Year parade with its flashy dragon and lion dances. Though it was fun, she always felt like a spectator of someone else's exotic red and gold "cultural" celebrations, and none of it brought her any closer to understanding her own heritage.

While the Chinatown version of Chinese American culture did not resonate with Natalie, neither did her mother's mahjong playing friends help to shed any light on what it meant to be Chinese. Their thinly disguised humble-talk about whose child was attending which prestigious university or who was successful as a doctor, engineer, or professor only made her painfully aware of her own useless liberal arts degree and lack of clear direction. Surely there was more to Chinese culture than the stereotypical emphasis on education, hard work, material success, and money.

In coming to China, Natalie hoped to clear away some of the

mistiness and to gain some insight into her parents' early childhoods before their families fled for Taiwan ahead of the Communist takeover in 1949. Studying qigong and its philosophy might help her understand the older China that her parents came from, a China that existed before much of its traditional culture was lost first to the leveling influences of Chinese communism with its many failed social and economic campaigns and now to the massive wave of modernization and rampant capitalism.

Master Zhu lived in a courtyard home not far from the Forbidden City in Beijing's old city center which was known for its historic but shrinking *hútong* districts. As Dāndān led the way through a maze of narrow *hútong* alleyways, some of which looked to be hundreds of years old, Natalie soon lost track of how many tight lanes they passed through. Working hard to build up her yoga business in its first year, she had not had many opportunities to explore her new home much less the oldest parts of Beijing. She saw now what she had been missing: taxis squeezed between cars parked on both sides of the *hútong* with just millimeters to spare, three-wheeled carts loaded high with produce rolled past vendor's stands, and men playing *xiàngqí* chess on low tables. Splayed-kneed cyclists casually skirted retirees in well-worn white tanks, and women in polyester prints strolled behind their snub-nosed lap dogs.

The traditional *hútong* architecture felt guarded and protective. No open lawns or exposed front doors here. Indeed, not much could be seen from within the narrow lanes, and everywhere Natalie looked her vision was blocked by the high, gray walls that shielded each family's inner courtyard from curious eyes. But tantalizing glimpses into recessed doorways revealed rusty bicycles propped against gray brick walls, sunlit walkways lined with pots of dusty vines, and waist-high white and blue Ming-style vases in which goldfish lazed among the trailing roots of water plants.

The entrance to Master Zhu's residence consisted of

a two-and-a-half-meter tall vermillion gate overhung with a sweeping tiled roof. Blue, green, and gold Qing dynasty-style *dǒugǒng*—interlocking wooden brackets that bore the weight of the roof on traditional Chinese structures—crowded the underside of the overhanging eaves, and an enormous inverted *fú* character for prosperity was carved right into the door's thick wood and painted a lustrous gold. The grand entrance was flanked on both sides by a pair of enormous stone lions. Clearly, Master Zhu was no ordinary Chinese citizen. Very few in China could afford to renovate a humble *hútong* dwelling into a place that was reminiscent of the lavish homes of officials and the scholar-nobility from a much older time.

Though Dāndān had led Natalie through the *hútongs* with confidence and ease, she became suddenly and inexplicably reserved when she pressed the electronic doorbell on the side of the grand gate. A smiling Master Zhu opened the door immediately as if he had been expecting them. He greeted them warmly and ushered them inside. Like many northern Chinese, he was tall and solidly built: his shoulders and chest were broad and round, and an ample belly stretched the front of an immaculate white dress shirt that was tucked neatly into black trousers. He did not look different from any other well-to-do, middle-aged man in Beijing and could have been an anonymous businessman or smug government official gliding by in one of the ubiquitous black Audis that cruised Beijing's streets, yet Natalie immediately understood Dāndān's reserve. Whatever his abilities were, merely his physical presence was intimidating enough. Surprisingly, however, Master Zhu was soft-spoken and mild-mannered—almost feminine and diffident in his gracious welcome.

The beauty of the inner courtyard stood in sharp contrast to the gray lane outside. A bean-shaped pool lined with smooth river rocks and a few masterfully placed jagged "cloud rocks" brightened the center of the rectangular space. Two willows trailed their branches into one end of the pond while neon-orange and smoky black koi fish wove languidly around water lily stalks beneath the trees' shade. The rounded, gentle green of the willows softened the vermillion of the pillars spaced evenly around the perimeter of the courtyard, and double wooden doors with latticed window panels like those found in temples opened onto living quarters on three sides.

The courtyard's high walls protected the pond's tranquility from the cacophony of the world outside, and the still air felt a little rarified, as if the courtyard were a small, enclosed ecosystem unto itself. The chaos of modern Beijing life would not disturb them here.

Master Zhu led Dāndān and Natalie to a large wooden table made from the hefty cross-section of a giant tree root and invited them to sit on low wooden stools. Simple and dainty implements for tea-making were already arranged neatly on the table: a wooden drip tray with carved edges held one large and one small ceramic teapot, tiny ceramic cups, a fine wire mesh strainer, and polished bamboo stir sticks and tongs. Nearby, an electric kettle was already whistling softly in readiness. Master Zhu took a seat behind the table. With fluid, graceful movements that seemed incongruent with his broad hands and thick fingers, he began to make tea. Every gesture was slow and deliberate, like a meditation: the initial warming of the ceramic ware, the rinsing of the tea leaves, the first steeping. Water poured over the ceramic ware darkened the curves of the teapot and cups before flowing out through elaborately carved holes in the drip tray.

As she watched the flowing water, Natalie was reminded of how simple life had been for her when she was a child. Her mother had given her an old teapot and cups of various sizes to play with in her bath. Left alone in the bathroom while her mother talked on the phone in the kitchen, she used the teapot to pour warm water into each of the cups, watching the cups overflow with the single-minded attention of the young. The simplicity of the tea ceremony and Master Zhu's concentration awakened in her the pleasure she had felt as that young child.

When Master Zhu handed Natalie a shot glass-sized teacup, she immediately recognized the woody aroma of a very fine *Pǔ'ěr* tea. Though normally an indiscriminate coffee drinker, Natalie was able to appreciate a fine tea thanks to her mother's influence, and she paused to savor the slightly bitter mouthful that left a faintly sweet impression on her tongue. This *Pǔ'ěr*, well-aged, probably fetched hundreds of yuan for a mere handful on the scale of a tea shop. Sipped slowly in Master Zhu's serene, immaculate courtyard, it was the perfect accompaniment to the man himself as if he, too, exuded the rich fragrance of a rare, well-aged tea.

"Dāndān has never introduced me to any of her friends so it is a distinct pleasure to meet you," Master Zhu said after they had enjoyed their first few fragrant sips in silence. "She told me you are interested in learning about qigong. What would you like to know?"

Natalie had so many questions she did not know where to start. The little she knew about qigong from her Western perspective was limited to a smattering of misleading impressions: sword-swallowing qigong masters whose insides were impervious to sharp edges; masters—or tricksters—who could move objects and bend spoons without touching them; the infamous Falun Gong movement and the subsequent crackdown by Chinese authorities. All her sources had been sensationalist TV documentaries and Hong Kong martial arts films viewed through a Western lens. Sensationalism notwithstanding, she wondered if the practice of certain kinds of qigong really did allow people to cultivate extraordinary abilities.

She had seen old people in slow, graceful movement as they practiced Taichi in city parks in the early morning sunshine. Qigong and its close cousin *Tàijíquán* were an integral part of traditional Chinese medicine, developed over thousands of years to help people stay healthy well into their golden years. Just as yoga had been developed for the select few in India, the age-old secrets of qigong had been reserved by grandmasters only for those who had proven themselves worthy, and most traditions had been transmitted strictly orally from master to student for thousands of years. As far as she could tell, there were definite similarities between yoga and qigong in theory, practice and tradition.

Natalie wanted to ask something intelligent and worthy of the qigong master's attention, but before she could formulate her first question he spoke again. He had been studying her with slightly narrowed eyes, his gaze focused somewhere on the mid-distance between them. "You have some stagnation in your liver and your kidneys are drained from trying to cool down an overheated heart. It is a long-standing condition, possibly congenital. Your *dāntián* is full of energy, though, and you do not lack drive." He paused, assessing. "You have an old injury on your right knee, and though it happened years ago it never fully healed. There is still a blockage near the front of the knee on the right." Natalie looked at Dāndān in bewilderment: how did he know about the knee she had injured in a bike accident when she was nine years old? Dāndān did not see her look, however, because she was gazing at Master Zhu with great admiration. Master Zhu continued calmly, "In Chinese culture, when an educated person views a sample of fine calligraphy, he understands the intent behind every brush stroke. Someone who is less refined sees only the characters as characters or he may even understand the deeper meaning behind the words. But one who is able to truly appreciate fine calligraphy knows that each stroke is infused with the spirit of the artist and his energy at the time the calligraphy was created. You are like a piece of calligraphy. It is not difficult to read you particularly as you are a trusting individual."

Whether she was trusting or naïve, Natalie felt as if he had effortlessly disarmed her and she was left completely exposed, her hands empty.

"Your knee still pains you sometimes?" he asked. Natalie nodded. "May I try something?" When Natalie nodded again, not knowing what she was agreeing to, Master Zhu raised his hands in front of him, palms facing her. He turned his gaze downward, and his eyelids drooped slightly as if he were about to go to sleep. Dāndān watched carefully from the side.

Her heart beating a little faster than usual, Natalie wondered what the man was trying to do but felt nothing out of the ordinary. Master Zhu held the position for several minutes, and when nothing happened, she relaxed. Just then, she felt a subtle tingling in her right knee. She wondered if it was her imagination, but the tingling was quickly followed by an intense heat as if someone were holding the red-hot tip of an iron poker to the exact spot that usually pained her in damp, cold weather or when she pushed herself too hard. To her complete bewilderment, she felt—could almost see in her mind's eye—the ligaments inside her knee *moving*, breaking through knots of scar tissue, and becoming correctly aligned. As her thoughts pinballed between doubt and awe, the tears began to fall in a stream. Soon, she was sobbing quietly, a great, inexplicable grief welling up inside of her.

Master Zhu remained still, holding the position. After some time, he lowered his hands and resumed the tea making, pouring more boiling water into the larger teapot for the next brewing. Dāndān looked thoughtful but said nothing while Natalie composed herself.

"Thank you," she said when she could speak again.

"It's nothing. You were ready for the healing."

"What did you do?"

Master Zhu grinned. "I gave you a small adjustment—that's all," he said, but even as he was speaking, his eyes were drawn to something behind them and his face changed. His gaze lingered as if something were commanding his attention against his will. Natalie and Dāndān both turned to look.

Standing just outside one of the double-paneled doors that led to the living quarters was a pudgy man in his mid-20s, about their age. His head was shaven and though he was almost as tall as Master Zhu, his clothes hung loosely on him as if both the t-shirt and nylon shorts were a size too large. His eyes were set just a little too closely together, the bridge of his piggish nose a little too flat, the jaw slack. While the flaccidness about his expression, his movements, and the too pale skin were disconcerting, what was most unsettling was his striking resemblance to Master Zhu as if, due to some dark cosmic prank, he was a loosely put together version of his father. He lacked more than just the self-possession and dignity of the older man, however.

"Ah, Xiǎo Gāng." Master Zhu's chuckle was choppy. "You know Dāndān. Come over and say hello. This is Dāndān's friend, *Nàtǎlì.*" The boy-man continued to stare at Natalie. She smiled but then immediately looked down at her hands as her fingers turned the rings around and around. Dāndān greeted Xiǎo Gāng in the exaggeratedly sweet tone that people use with very young children, but she also looked away immediately and began to study the glossy tabletop. Master Zhu busied himself with the tea making implements, but his movements were not as fluid as before. The tongs slipped from his fingers and fell with a clatter onto the wooden drip tray. He picked them up, clearing his throat. "Xiǎo Gāng has been studying qigong since he was four. He's quite accomplished for someone his age and given his, ah, limitations." Xiǎo Gāng, hearing his name, glanced in his father's direction but continued to stare at Natalie, studying every detail about her: the wild hair, the tight-fitting yoga top, and the multiple piercings. He seemed particularly intrigued by the way the rainbow of stones on her rings caught and threw off the sunlight as her fingers fidgeted in her lap. "Would you like some tea?" his father asked, but Xiǎo Gāng continued to ignore him. He moved a little closer so he could see the rings better. "He likes things that sparkle," Master Zhu said, clearing his throat again.

Natalie tried to relax her fingers as Xiǎo Gāng continued to scrutinize her. "If you don't mind my asking," she said, trying to ignore the discomfort she felt, "the adjustment you did for me—is it a skill that can be learned or is it an innate ability?"

"Some of it I was born with, but most of it came about through diligent practice. My father was a great qigong master. He began teaching me when I was three." Master Zhu's hands became still, and he did not speak for several moments. When he continued, his voice had become a little hoarse. "I was only a boy when he died. Things were very chaotic in China at that time. There were so many things I did not understand as a child."

"It is unfortunate that you lost your father at a young age. It's admirable, however, that you have been able to carry on the tradition."

Master Zhu said nothing for such a long time that Natalie wondered if she had offended him. When he continued, it was as if he were speaking more to himself, his voice heavy with regret. "The whole country was overtaken by madness. We were so scared. We were so terrified of being caught on the wrong side that we—" he had trouble finishing the sentence. "Even my father could not protect me when they targeted him. I was only doing as he instructed when I distanced myself from him to save myself. I don't know if even he knew that things would get so out of control. I can't help but wonder if he would still be alive if I had not obeyed him." He looked up, not bothering to hide his sadness. "Carrying on the tradition was the least I could do in honor of my father's memory even though it was not easy in those days to be a qigong practitioner. Many qigong masters died, left the country, or went into hiding. I hid my practice for many years."

Natalie had studied the Cultural Revolution briefly in college. While she did not remember names and dates, her general impression of the time was that it had been a period of great social upheaval which Chairman Máo used to consolidate his power within the Chinese Community Party after the disastrous economic and political failures of his Great Leap Forward campaign in the 1950s. Máo shrewdly tapped into the idealism, naïveté and hot emotions of the country's youth by calling on them to rebel against virtually everything, as it were, in order to achieve his goal of ousting his enemies within the Party and thus seizing control for himself once again. During the frenzy of the country-wide revolution, neighbors reported neighbors, colleagues turned on each other, and children betrayed their own parents. The violence of that time destroyed physical structures—cultural and historical sites and artifacts, personal property, temples, churches, and monasteries—as well as traditional familial and societal bonds that had formed the foundation of Chinese society for thousands of years.

Master Zhu's words hinted of great personal pain and Natalie wanted to ask him what it had been like to live through such a momentous time in history, but plainly it was still a very sensitive subject for him. She and Dāndān sat in respectful silence until Master Zhu straightened up and applied himself once again to the tea-making. The moment had passed. Pouring more tea into Natalie's small teacup, he asked briskly, "You are interested in studying qigong? I understand you are a yoga teacher. From what Dāndān has told me, it seems like a good form of exercise. I'd like to know if you work with the vital qi energy in yoga. Conscious circulation of qi is one of the fundamental aspects of any qigong practice."

"I believe there are correlations in yoga practice," Natalie began slowly. She was still feeling wooly headed from the healing, and she had so many questions about Master Zhu's fatherless childhood, but something about what he said or the way he said it did not sit well with her. It took her some effort to formulate a response. "Though many yoga teachers teach only the physical aspects of yoga, more traditional yogis practice pranayama. Pranayama is breathwork that helps one circulate life-force energy in the body. I think prana is very similar to qi. We may use different techniques, but I think the principles behind the practices are similar."

Master Zhu nodded. "When I scanned your energy field, I saw many places where your qi is stagnant. How is it that your 'breathing exercises,' as a teacher of yoga, have not cleared the stagnation?" It was a reasonable question and his interest appeared to be a purely academic one, but Natalie felt attacked. She knew that she should practice more pranayama and sitting meditation, but she had never been drawn to the less rigorous and less physically demanding aspects of yoga. She breathed when she practiced, she reasoned, and asana practice itself was already a moving meditation. Natalie did not know how to answer the qigong master without letting her irritation show so she forced herself to smile and sit up straighter as she resorted to a tactic that had helped her in the past with Chinese people: false humility. "I am a young teacher. I still have a lot to learn about yoga which, like qigong, can be a life-long practice. I am still only a student myself."

Master Zhu smiled. "True enough!" he exclaimed. "There is always room for us to improve." He was about to say more but Xiǎo Gāng, who had been inching closer to the tree root table, spoke up.

"I practice qigong. Father makes me practice three hours every day."

"Yes, Xiǎo Gāng is quite good," Master Zhu said without looking at his son. "Even someone like him can practice qigong with good results."

"Does *āyí* practice qigong?"

"*Āyí* is a teacher of yoga. She is interested in studying qigong." It was subtle, to be sure, but everything Master Zhu said in his smooth, modulated voice seemed to imply that qigong was superior to yoga, that his discipline was superior to hers.

"I think the two traditions operate on the same principles and are only different in form," Natalie said hotly. She was aware that she could not back up any of what she was saying since she knew very little about qigong, but it was too late to stop now. "Obviously, there might be some superficial differences, but that's natural because they developed within different cultural contexts."

"Maybe so," the qigong master replied with the same easy smile. "If what you say is true, why don't we try something, a small test of your hypothesis? If yoga is as powerful as qigong, then you should have no difficulty with a simple exercise that all qigong practitioners are familiar with. Xiǎo Gāng, please demonstrate how the Horse Stance is practiced."

An immediate change came over Xiǎo Gāng. His eyes became focused and his body drew itself up with an intelligent grace as he placed his feet a careful shoulder's distance apart. Holding his arms in front of him as if he were gently hugging a large tree trunk, he bent his knees deeply while keeping his back straight. He looked like he was perched on the edge of an imaginary chair. It was just the same as *Utkatasana*. Before she could think about what she was doing, Natalie had jumped up from her stool and was bending her knees into Chair pose, holding her arms in front of her to make Chair into Horse. Though she had taught three classes a day every day this week and her legs were already sore, she knew that the key to standing squats was to tuck her tailbone, engage her core, and relax the backs of her legs. Natalie relaxed her arms, her face and her legs. She focused her gaze on a teacup resting on the glossy surface of the tree root table and willed herself to breathe more slowly.

The storm in her head made it difficult to concentrate, but the hours she had spent on the mat were paying off: through sheer force of habit, her breathing gradually slowed into a long *ujjayi* breath. Natalie realized how upset she was only after she had begun to breathe: master or no master, it was incredibly arrogant and ignorant of him to automatically assume superiority of one tradition over another. The weight and authority of thousands of years of development and practice stood behind yoga just as it did qigong. Why was there a need, moreover, to pit one tradition against the other or to consider them mutually exclusive?

A minute passed in the still courtyard. The tall gray walls felt at once protective and oppressive. All that happened in a courtyard such as this one would always remain unknown to the outside world. Maybe that was why the Chinese built their walls so high.

As the minutes continued to tick by and Natalie continued to breathe, the wild thoughts began to settle. She continued to breathe, and the courtyard melted into a timeless space. The feeling of oppression lifted, bit by bit. Just as the intense heat of a forest fire is nothing compared to the Earth's molten core, the rash heat that had spiked up within her was being engulfed by a very different kind of fire: *this* power originated from the very center of her being, and it gave her the ability to stand indefinitely. As the new fire moved through her and burned away the last traces of anger and the chaotic tangle of thoughts, all that was left was the pose, her breath and the teacup. This is what the ancient yogis meant by *Utkatasana*: powerful pose.

Master Zhu's expression remained inscrutable as he observed the pair before him: Natalie's figure mirroring Xiǎo Gāng's larger one, two static lightning bolts in profile beside a still pond. Dāndān hardly breathed as she looked from Natalie to Xiǎo Gāng and back to Natalie again, her face a read of admiration, anticipation and excitement.

Xiǎo Gāng had started out strongly enough, but as the minutes wore on his legs began to tremble a little. The more they shook, the more his gaze wavered, and soon his face was screwed up with effort. Finally, face strained red, he stood up abruptly, pounding his thighs violently with his fists. Natalie held steady for a few more long breaths then straightened up gracefully, smiling. She had been standing for almost ten minutes. Dāndān clapped and threw her arms around her friend.

"Ah, Xiǎo Gāng, you have made me lose face," Master Zhu said with a small deprecating smile. Xiǎo Gāng paced the courtyard, wiping sweat from his forehead with both hands as he muttered incoherently, eyes avoiding his father's face.

"You did well, Xiǎo Gāng," Dāndān said belatedly. "How can you expect to compete against a teacher?" But the more Xiǎo Gāng paced, head down, the more agitated he became. Turning abruptly, tears streaming down his face, he ran out of the courtyard. The large red doors slammed shut behind him.

"Is he OK?" Natalie asked, but Master Zhu did not even glance at the doors.

"He always goes over to Grandma Wú's place when he's upset. It's fine—cautious animals never stray far."

It took Natalie a few moments to absorb the animal reference. "Who is Grandma Wú?"

"My next-door neighbor. She's harmless enough though some people—the old and the superstitious—claim she's some sort of healer. She's never received any formal training in either conventional or traditional Chinese medicine as far as I know. She certainly did not study qigong with any reputable teachers so I'm skeptical. But whatever the case, she came back from Inner Mongolia in the '80s a changed person. Ever heard of the term *Ménggǔ dàifu*, a Mongol healer? That's what we Chinese call charlatans. Our own Grandma Wú just might be a bona fide Mongol healer!" He chortled at his own joke, smiling broadly to himself even after the laughter had died away.

"*Nàtǎlì* is quite good!" Dāndān broke in, her arm still draped around Natalie's waist. "Maybe yoga and qigong are not so different after all."

"Not bad," he replied, but that was all he said for several minutes as he sipped slowly from a tiny teacup, a small smile on his face. "It appears you have a good foundation," he finally said, turning to Natalie. "I do not accept many students these days, but I am willing to teach you, and I am willing to teach you all that I know. I have been waiting for a student like you for a long time."

Dāndān gave a small gasp of understanding and was already

offering Natalie her congratulations before Natalie fully grasped his meaning. It would be a dream come true if she could study with a teacher like Master Zhu—a once in a lifetime opportunity. Not many Westerners had the language skills or the chance to study with a real qigong master in China. Given her experience today with both the healing and with *Utkatasana* which proved that her knee had indeed healed, Natalie was more curious than ever about qigong's possibilities. Flattered and gratified, Natalie accepted Master Zhu's offer to teach her all that he knew.

*"I don't know what I was expecting when I came to Beijing two years ago," the young woman says. "I had a dream of teaching yoga, of studying qigong, but all that is gone now."*

*"When I was your age, I had so many dreams too. I was very idealistic. Then I lost everything," Wú replies.*

*The young woman collects their plates and washes them at the sink while the older woman uses a clean cloth to cover the rest of the shāobǐng with their light, flaky crusts.*

# The Non-Incident



Mongolian women are forbidden to watch when men slaughter animals. But I was not a Mongolian woman, and the continuous bawling of a goat drew me inexorably to a spot behind the compound fence where I could watch undetected. I had a morbid desire to know what happened when they killed an animal. I needed to know how they did it. The ineffectual lurching of the tightly bound limbs and the helplessness of an animal thrown onto its back felt very immediate and very relevant just then. I watched the rolling eyes, heard the shrieks, and felt the animal's desperation in my own body. Unlike sheep who struggle without sound, goats are spirited fighters to the last breath.

The men moved quickly and efficiently in their work, cigarettes dangling loosely from the corners of their mouths. After a long-bladed knife had been sharpened on a rough stone and smoothed against a leather strop, a precise incision was made right below the animal's sternum. One of the men held the goat's snout firmly closed while another pinned the jerking legs to the ground. The first man widened the incision and, rolling up the sleeve of his *deel*, inserted his hand and most of his forearm into the chest cavity. The animal was still alive, its screams muffled.

How detached they were. I imagined that the body they held down was not that of a goat's but a young woman's. Maybe one or several of the men so matter-of-factly slaughtering the goat right now had been there last night. There was no way for me to know.

Mercifully, death came quickly for the goat. The man's hand was still inside of her when she began sighing her last, long, rasping breaths. Then she was only a carcass.

The men called out gruffly to the women for a basin into which they tossed the purplish red organs and intestines marbled with lacelike fat. Then they used a small ceramic rice bowl to scoop out the blood pooling in the body cavity before it could congeal. I was transfixed by the contrast of vermillion on white as blood streamed down the sides of the bowl. When the animal's bowels were empty, the men finished skinning the body and, working their knife points neatly and rapidly between the joints, they deftly disassembled what had been a living, breathing being just moments before. I had yet to see a Mongolian break or cut through an animal's bones. They respected the integrity of animal bone, but a woman's soft flesh was a different matter.

I turned away from the hole in the fence. I knew what to expect from this point on: the women would clean the stomach and intestines with river water before stuffing them with pieces of meat and fat. Lengths of the small intestines would be filled with a blood and flour mixture for blood sausages. Normally I would have stayed to help in this work, but today I needed to go to the township center, my mind a jumble of words I would use to defend my friend's honor. I could not, however, shake the feeling of already being defeated before I had begun.

Dorj's eyes flitted up briefly when I entered the Brigade Headquarters, but the Brigade Leader immediately returned her attention to the papers on her desk. She gave no indication that she had seen me other than to frown at the documents in front of her. Not knowing what to do, I stood awkwardly in front of her as I waited for her to acknowledge my presence. She let me stand there for a full minute.

"What do you want, Comrade Wú?" She finally said without looking up. Her eyes continued to scan the documents. If it had not been for me, Xiǎomèi would not have been sent to this barbarian land. Maybe she would have been somewhere warmer or at least in a place where the locals were friendlier. I cleared my throat.

"There was an incident last night that involved two of the students from Beijing," I began.

"Yes, I heard something," Dorj said noncommittally, cutting me off. Of course she already knew about the incident. News travels faster than a grassland fire in a small town, but as Brigade Leader she had not offered us any assistance even when she knew that something had happened. Suddenly, a hot anger filled me that gave me the strength I needed to speak up for Xiǎomèi, to speak up for all of us.

"Two of our students were attacked and beaten by a group of local men. One managed to run away from the attackers but the other was brutally...brutally..." I did not know how to finish the sentence. If it had been the other girl or myself—we were stronger—but how could I even think such a thing? Several Mongolian men on horseback had descended upon the two students who were on foot. Their breaths had reeked of alcohol. They let Poet run away, but Xiǎomèi had not been as fortunate.

"The two were out late past their curfew," Dorj said. Her eyes were cold when she finally looked up. I tried to look her in the eye, but my resolve quickly crumbled in the face of her deep contempt, and I realized that I was a very young woman who had no experience dealing with forces much greater than herself.

"The boy was walking the girl home," I stammered. "They were working late helping with the preparations. For the official visit." The goat they just slaughtered was for officials visiting from Hohhot.

"How do we know there were others involved?" Dorj asked. "My understanding of the situation is that something happened between the two students—a lover's quarrel for all I know—and the boy ran away after he had taught the girl a lesson. There were no witnesses."

This, then, was to be the official version of events. Dorj was going to protect the Mongolian men at all costs. I realized then how foolish I had been to think that we would get any sympathy much less help from the local government. Though Dorj had, through official obligation, gone through the motions of welcoming us when we first arrived, she had made it very clear from the beginning that we were not wanted. She had expressed her disdain in subtle ways: a missed report here, a misplaced request there, feigned misunderstandings. For the local government, we were an extra responsibility and liability they could just as well have done without.

I did not understand at the time that Dorj had good reason to resent our presence. Her ancestors' nomadic way of life was rapidly being undermined by the arrival of more and more agrarian-minded Han Chinese settlers in the area. With the formation of production teams, brigades and newly imposed agrarian endeavors, the traditional Mongolian way of life was undergoing an irrevocable and largely unwelcomed transformation. As assets and resources were collectivized, age-old clans and alliances were broken up by the formation of communes. Herders whose ancestors had roamed the grasslands for countless centuries were forced to settle in townships. Local religious practices were banned, the clergy were persecuted, and temples were ransacked. As a newly arrived outsider, I did not grasp the implications of what our presence meant to the people who were already living in what the Han Chinese considered to be frontier land, nor did I understand the gravity of the changes that were taking place around me. All I knew was that the site of our exile was bitterly cold, unwelcoming, and dangerous. I pressed on not realizing that I was, in my persistence, chafing an open wound.

"As one of the senior comrades in the group," I said, trying to stand up taller, "I need to make a thorough report of the incident, and I want to press charges on behalf of the students who were attacked last night."

"That's ludicrous," Dorj snapped. "How are you going to 'press charges' when there were no witnesses to a non-incident?" She eyed me for a few long moments before deciding that I was not worth the trouble. She sighed. "This is a personal matter between two comrades who quarreled and had a falling out. That's all. This matter does not concern the Brigade Headquarters."

I wavered for a moment as the dark fear from the night before washed over me again. The five of us from Beijing had been helping to decorate the town meeting hall for the upcoming Spring Festival celebrations, or, as the locals called it, *Tsagaan Sar.* Though winter was not yet over, the holiday heralded a new year ahead, and it was a relief for us to be working indoors on something cheerful. Our banter and laughter filled the banquet hall as we hung up dozens of strings of red lanterns and created banners with new year well wishes and revolutionary slogans. As the evening progressed, the other students and I finally noticed that Poet somehow always managed to find a place next to Xiǎomèi: he was there offering her a hand up the ladder, bringing her more string, running to fetch the scissors for her. I smiled to myself as I bent over the calligraphy I was writing on a wide, red banner. In the first few months of our exile, we had not managed to make many friends among the locals so we stayed together as much as possible. After spending every day together for weeks on end, we had come to know each other very well. We knew who was the most hardworking, the most adventurous, the one who could make anyone laugh, the one who missed home the most. Poet was a shy, studious young man who was not bad looking in spite of his thick glasses. Polite almost to a fault, there was much to like about his quiet, thoughtful manner. Given the fact that none of us knew how long we would be in the countryside, he was not, after all, a bad match for Xiǎomèi who needed someone who could appreciate her quick wit and intelligence but who also would not be gruff or overbearing with her.

Xiǎomèi did not seem to mind that he was constantly by her side. She kept her eyes on what she was doing, but I noticed that she kept glancing over at him when she thought he wasn't looking. Once or twice, he caught her sneaking peeks and they both looked away quickly, blushing all the way up to their hairlines. When neither of them were looking, the other students and I migrated to the other side of the hall to hang decorations, exchanging knowing smiles between us. We were all in good spirits, for in the midst of a very long and cold first winter, it felt good to be doing something festive even while it made us homesick for our families and the city.

At the end of the evening, Xiǎomèi and Poet wanted to stay on just a little longer to put a few finishing touches on the decorations, so the other two students and I went on without them, winking to each other. We were almost as giddy about the budding romance as they were. It helped to take our minds off the hard work and drudgery that now characterized our daily lives.

When it got to be very late and Xiǎomèi still had not returned, the other girl and I began to worry. As the town hall was only a twenty-minute walk from our *ger*, we wondered if they had gotten to talking and had forgotten the time. But it was far past midnight, and both came from respectable families who had raised them with good manners. They knew that too much time spent alone together would cause people to talk even if we were far away from our families and communities in Beijing. By one o'clock, we knew that something was very wrong: Xiǎomèi would never stay out so late with a boy. All the fears I had been collecting from the time we arrived flooded over me: fear of being attacked by wolves, fear of freezing to death in the middle of the night, fear of failing to be re-educated, fear of the very starkness of the snow-covered grassland that could suck the life out of us within minutes. The other girl and I looked at each other, neither of us brave enough to voice our fears. Without speaking, we hurried into our thick winter *deels* and boots and headed back to the town hall.

It did not take us long to find Xiǎomèi. She was curled up on the side of the road, clutching the folds of her torn *deel,* and shuddering violently. She had been too hurt to drag herself the half kilometer home and would have died in the deep cold if we had not found her when we did.

"I am going now to see the Chief of Public Security," I said to Dorj.

"Do what you feel is best, Comrade, but you are wasting your time. The Chief Inspector has many more important matters to attend to." Dorj turned back to the papers on her desk, dismissing me.

"Brigade Leader." The defeat and desperation in my voice sounded pathetic to my own ears. Dorj sighed loudly but did not look up.

"Our comrade requires medical attention that is beyond what the local clinic can provide. Do I have your permission to accompany her to the Bayan Nuur hospital? We will both be absent from work for a few days." Dorj looked up then with narrowed eyes but said nothing. She briskly filled out a leave of absence form and even arranged to have us transported to the hospital by jeep. A death in the township would not reflect well on her either.

Xiǎomèi survived. Though not strong physically, my friend had a will of iron. Who would have guessed there were such reserves of strength beneath that delicate surface? I stayed by her bedside for three weeks, sleeping beneath her cot at night on bedding I had brought with us. The hospital was short-staffed, ill-equipped, and lacking even the most basic medicines. The effects of the Cultural Revolution had been far-reaching indeed, for even this far from the political epicenter many of the local doctors had been struggled against and expelled from the hospital, leaving only a handful of poorly trained nursing students whose blundering efforts were focused on patients whose conditions were even more critical than Xiǎomèi's. It fell on me to sponge bathe her, administer the antibiotics prescribed to her, bring her food that I procured with my own meal tickets, and empty her chamber pot.

Though I worried about the safety of the students who remained in the countryside, the long days we spent in the barren hospital gave me a lot of time to think and wrestle with the countless emotions that washed over me: guilt, anger, helplessness, despair, grief. Dealing with my own emotions proved difficult enough, but witnessing Xiǎomèi's struggle to hang on to this world was all but unbearable. There was nothing I could do but watch and wait.

"*Dàjiě*, I can't thank you enough for taking care of me," she whispered when she finally awoke from the fever that raged through her for a full week. Heart in my throat, I stroked the hair away from her face and did not know what to say. She looked so young, lying there, still just a child, and I was only a little older. How could either of us know what we were supposed to do in such a situation? I raised a soup spoon to her dry lips.

"Try to eat a little. Build up your strength." She shook her head and broth trickled from the corner of her mouth. I wiped it away with a rag.

"It's not the pain. It's not my body. I think I could almost walk now if I tried," she said. I put the spoon down and stroked her hand. As I waited for her to finish the thought, the exhaustion I had not allowed myself to feel descended on me all at once, and I felt as if I would never be able to get up from the metal stool next to her bed. Just a few days ago my former self would have peppered her with questions or pressed her to speak, but now I remembered something Shīfu had told his students once: sometimes the best gift we can give someone who is hurting is our silent presence. It was several long days of silence before Xiǎomèi spoke again.

The days we spent in the hospital ran together into a blur of fatigue and ennui. Day after day, the hazy winter sunlight streamed through the south-facing window by Xiǎomèi's bed. As I dozed in a chair next to her, I noticed that every time I opened my eyes the panes of sunlight on the floor had shifted a couple more centimeters towards the east. That was the only change in the room as Xiǎomèi and the other patients lay on their metal cots. I struggled against the stillness of the room and against the days of inactivity, feeling a quiet despair come over me. What did I want, I asked myself. I could not return to Beijing, and even if I were to return who knew what state I would find the city in? Schools and universities were still closed, and though people tried to lead normal lives, sporadic violence still broke out here and there so people were never sure when it would erupt again. The letters I exchanged with a handful of close friends had, by the fifth month of our exile, become few and far in between. We did not know if our letters were opened by the authorities or even if they reached their intended recipients. With nothing positive to report, we wrote infrequently. When my friends did write, I sensed their deep disappointment behind the sanguine greetings. I am sure they sensed the same in my short missives to them.

Young and in my prime, I had come to the countryside with an abundance of energy and ideals. Not only was there nothing of significance for us to accomplish out on the frontier far from the civilized world, but we now found ourselves infinitely vulnerable in our isolation. Was this how we were to spend the rest of our lives? Collecting frozen dung to fuel the fire? Squatting like an animal out on the open grassland when we needed to relieve ourselves? Constantly looking over our shoulders for men on horseback?

"I cannot face my family," Xiǎomèi said one day, rousing me from my troubled ruminations.

"There's no need to tell them," I said but without conviction. We both knew there was no way we could hide something like this. People are fascinated by violence and are drawn to tragedy even when they have no intention of helping. More likely than not the whole township knew about the attack by now, and as far away as Beijing was, people there would find out sooner or later. What was worse, I wondered, the fear or the shame? One was a ghost that occupied her heart while the other disfigured like a jagged scar on her face that she would wear for the rest of her life. Xiǎomèi had a will of iron, but in that barren place we found ourselves, what did she have to live for? What did any of us have to live for?

# Trip to Cuàndǐxia

BEIJING, 2005

"How would you like to come with me to the countryside tomorrow?" Malcolm asked Natalie one cool fall morning. The gingko trees lining Beijing's broad boulevards were just beginning to change from a soft green to a brilliant yellow. In a few weeks, the bright yellow fans would carpet the sidewalks like soft gold. "There's a small village called Cuàndǐxia that's not too far from Beijing, but I hear it's like the village is frozen in time. Some of the best-preserved *sìhéyuàn* in northern China are in Cuàndǐxia, and many of these courtyard homes are over 400 years old. We could spend the night. Experience living history."

While Malcolm's work often took him away from home, one thing Natalie loved about being his new housemate and business partner was that he was always willing to show her the Beijing that he knew, providing her with an insider's view of the city. Ever casual though a touch paternalistic, he had taken it upon himself to play host whenever he returned from business trips, brushing off her many thanks with a shrug. With a guide like Malcolm, Natalie saw a lot of the city she never would have discovered on her own: newly opened minority cuisine restaurants, hole-in-the-wall Beijing eateries, an artists' colony that had blossomed in an old factory complex. This, however, was the first time he had offered to take her somewhere where they would spend the night. The idea appealed to her. She longed to get away from the crushing crowds and pollution of the city if only for a night or two. And it would just be the two of them.

"Oh—one thing. The village does have running water and electricity, but the infrastructure is a bit dated. I hear they only have outdoor toilets. Can you handle that?" Malcolm asked solicitously.

Natalie snorted. "I think, city boy, the question is not whether I can handle it, but whether *you* can handle it."

"Oh and...in the countryside the squat toilets are communal. Sometimes they leave the doors off the stalls."

"I love an adventure," she replied. It was decided then. They would leave the next day.

When they arrived at the gate to the village, a young guard greeted them apologetically. "I'm sorry, sir, but the village is full. You're welcome to walk around while there's some daylight left," he said, squinting at the western sky which was still a bright orange. "But all the guest rooms have been reserved for the night due to the national holiday. If you wish to spend the night somewhere close by, there's a hotel in Zhāitáng."

Malcolm frowned. They had seen the hotel on the way up. A blockish, chipped paint throw-back to much earlier and much less prosperous times, it was clearly not an option for Malcolm. He stepped out of the car and casually offered the guard a cigarette, his eyes scanning the steep sides of the valley with their terraced fields, the stone walls bordering the uneven, stone-lined road that led into the center of the village, the gray-tiled rooftops of houses set carefully into the steep mountainside.

"Why don't you ask again," he said to the guard, handing him a one thousand yuan note. The young guard looked flustered. "That's for the toll," Malcolm added, still surveying the village ahead of them. The guard asked if he had any smaller bills, but Malcolm waved him on. Looking dubious, the young man returned to the guardhouse to find change. They could see him through the window consulting his superior and gesturing with the one thousand yuan note. The older man glanced over at Malcolm's shiny black Audi and picked up the phone. Not ten minutes later, the young guard was waving them into Cuàndǐxia with a huge smile and a smart salute. Both he and Malcolm seemed to have forgotten about the change for the one thousand yuan.

The middle-aged hostess for the courtyard home was so effusive in her welcome that she had come out to the road to greet and usher them inside. Natalie had noticed a while ago that Malcolm inspired such treatment without needing to say a word: he was a man in his prime and clearly a wealthy and successful one at that. In a wolf pack, he would have been the sleek alpha male.

After the first cursory up-and-down look at Natalie, the woman directed all that she had to say to Malcolm though she did glance at Natalie once or twice with a small frown. When the frown deepened, Natalie realized she had been written off as a prostitute or mistress at best. She had toned down her jewelry for their countryside adventure and had woven her unruly mane into a demure, loose braid, but the shoulder-baring spaghetti straps on her yoga top and her tiny diamond nose stud in particular received stern, disapproving looks.

When the woman finally hurried off to attend to her other guests, Malcolm and Natalie stood in the doorway of the tiny room they were to share for the night. Lit by a single fluorescent tube above a rickety table, the room was cast in a cold, blue light that accentuated the shabbiness of the scant furnishings. A hot water thermos and two inverted glasses stood forlornly on a dented metal tray on a small table opposite the door. Two metal stools were stacked beneath the table, and the rest of the room was taken up by an expansive *kàng,* the traditional sleeping platform.

Malcolm glanced at Natalie and cleared his throat. "If this arrangement is not acceptable to you," he began, indicating the *kàng* with its limp red and pink cotton bedding folded neatly at the foot of the bed, "we can go back to the city. Who knew the village would be so crowded. Guess word has gotten out about Cuàndǐxia."

Natalie looked at Malcolm in surprise. The Malcolm she had come to know these past few months was, invariably, the ever confident, slightly indulgent alpha male who enjoyed showing the bumbling Chinese American around town. The hint of vulnerability that the novel environment brought out in him was intriguing. Though the single *kàng* meant they would be sharing a bed that night, it was spacious enough for three or four adults. She smiled and shrugged. "If you can handle the sleeping arrangement, I don't have any problems with it."

Malcolm chuckled with relief. "If you were a typical Chinese woman, I'd be sleeping in the car tonight!" It was somehow very gratifying that he did not lump her in with other Chinese women.

Malcolm lifted up a corner of the bedding to show her the *kàng's* construction. Perhaps as old as Chinese civilization itself, at least in the harsh north, the *kàng* was the warm heart of every Chinese home: people socialized, created families, died and mourned their dead on the *kàng*. Made of brick or baked clay, the platform bed had a built-in stove with maze-like flues that ran beneath the bricks in an ingenious design that kept families warm on long winter nights.

When they swung open the metal door to the stove, Natalie was relieved to see that there was already a fire burning briskly inside. She had not realized the countryside would be so much colder than the city and had been shivering ever since they left the warmth of the car. It was a relief to know that they would be warm that night even if the kitschy pink and floral Hello Kitty décor left a lot to be desired. But it was very Chinese: Natalie could imagine their hostess picking out bedding that in her mind was charming and cheerful.

Still smiling, Malcolm steered her back to the main courtyard of the compound where a few small folding metal tables had been set up. The compound's other guests were drinking beer and snacking on roasted peanuts while they waited for their meals.

Seeing them, the hostess immediately bustled over with a metal teapot, two white teacups, and small plates of pickled cabbage and peanuts on a tray. Still ignoring Natalie, she handed a small, dog-eared, hand-penned menu to Malcolm.

"Only humble country fare, I'm afraid," she said. "But everything is grown or caught locally." Malcolm barely glanced at the menu.

"What would you recommend, Older Sister?"

"The fish is very fresh—caught just this morning from the stream below the village. We can steam it with ginger, garlic, green onions and soy sauce. Or we can fry it with garlic and chilies from our garden. Guests from the city often enjoy the mushrooms and wild mountain greens—they're a local specialty. We harvest the greens in the summertime and preserve them the traditional way by drying and salting them. The mushrooms are gathered by hand right in these hills."

Malcolm pretended to consider the options, taking a slow sip from his teacup. "The tea is quite good," he said, spitting a small twig fragment into his hand.

"So pleased you like it, sir. There are only certain weeks in the springtime when we can harvest the leaves up in the mountains. Every household in the village has their own blend, but we mix a few secret ingredients into our tea to make it the healthiest and most flavorful tea in the whole village. It will keep you young and in your prime for a long time to come."

Natalie watched the exchange with a mixture of amusement and exasperation. Uninhibited and direct at home, the public Malcolm, she had noticed a while ago, was a deliberate, slow-speaking individual who did not mind making others wait for him. He took it for granted, as was the case with their hostess, that people would fall all over themselves to serve him.

"Would the gentleman like something to drink besides tea? We have room temperature and chilled beer—Yānjīng, Tsingdao and Tiger. We also have Èrguōtóu and a selection of fine *báijiǔ*—Máotái,

Wŭliángyè, Gŭyuè Lóngshān.... We're a humble little village, but we try to treat our guests well." Pretending to pore over the hand-written menu she could not read, Natalie raised her eyebrows: *báijiŭ*—white spirits. The ubiquitous, clear, 50 to 110 proof liquor that smelled and tasted like paint thinner was as essential to Chinese social functions as tea. Imbibed and vomited in large quantities at banquets and celebrations, *báijiŭ* was the grease that kept the social cogs turning in China. The cheaper stuff was sold in large plastic jugs with pop-off caps while the high-end stuff sold for hundreds if not thousands of yuan.

Malcolm took in Natalie's look with amusement. "My friend does not drink—she is a teacher," he informed the woman. "I'm not much of a drinker either. The tea is fine."

He did that sometimes. He did not usually consult her when they went out together—it had something to do with the fact that he was the host and was quite a few years older than she—yet he was always looking out for her in that watchful way of his. Malcolm had noticed the woman's treatment of Natalie so had dropped a comment that would help their hostess place Natalie socially above herself. Although she was perfectly capable of speaking for herself, even in Mandarin, Natalie appreciated this alert quality in Malcolm despite the deceptively sleepy eyes. He missed very little.

Suddenly solicitous, the hostess turned to Natalie with a bright, fake smile. "Would *xiǎojiě* like some juice or a soda?"

Malcolm ordered the fish and, mindful that Natalie was a vegetarian, ordered several vegetable dishes. After he had sent their hostess away, Natalie leaned towards him, her crossed forearms resting on the metal table. The flagstones that their table was resting on had sunk deep into the ground over the years and the table tilted precariously towards Natalie.

"At the gate," she said as Malcolm found a small triangular stone to wedge beneath the table leg, "the guard didn't give you change for the thousand."

"It was a tip for their kind help," he said, testing the table's stability.

"Nine hundred ninety yuan...that's almost 130 US dollars. That's a pretty big tip. People don't usually leave tips in China." For a moment, Natalie was not even sure Malcolm was listening as, satisfied with the table and back in his seat now, his gaze swept casually across the courtyard surveying the other diners.

"We would not be sitting here in this pleasant courtyard enjoying mountain tea. It's the way things are done in China," he finally said.

"Bribing guards? Under the table dealings?"

"The only table I've been doing business under is this one," he smiled. Then seeing her expression, he turned to face her and continued in a more serious tone. "It's the way things have always been done here, and I believe this is how things always will be. It's human nature for people to use what advantages they have. Because if they don't, someone else will."

"That's what capitalists say when they try to rationalize their exploitation of the less fortunate. China is supposed to be a Communist country."

"You're very young, little American. You're very naïve."

"I may be naïve, but I know what I see."

"And what do you see?" His eyes were dispassionate. Then he looked away. Natalie faltered. She had never seen this side of Malcolm, and it intimidated her. She did not want to argue with him, but she also could not ignore her sense of justice.

"You can say what you want about me being an American," Natalie said, "but at least in my country there is respect for the law. Without laws, there can be no order in society."

"Maybe most Americans are law-abiding citizens. I do believe that although I have never been to America myself. Most all of the Americans I have met are rather naïve, like yourself. Even the older ones." Natalie opened her mouth to protest but he stopped her with an upheld hand. "Do the top politicians and capitalists in your country abide by the law? Why do we in other countries hear about major corporate scandals in America? Shady dealings in the top rungs of government? I saw a very interesting movie recently by an American filmmaker—I think it was called *Fahrenheit 9/11*." While one could find pirated versions of virtually any movie in China, from Hollywood blockbusters to obscure foreign films, Natalie was surprised that Malcolm would be interested in much less watch Michael Moore's latest docudrama.

"The movie makes some interesting points," she conceded.

"Do you honestly believe that, on a certain level, things are so different between China and the US?"

Natalie stopped to consider the question. She grasped his point, but the conversation was not going in a direction she liked. She struggled to understand the discomfort she had felt in seeing him pass the guard the one thousand yuan note, but what he said was true. If he had not "tipped" the guards, they would not be sitting here enjoying the village and the beautiful food their hostess was now setting down in front of them: a whole steamed fish, stir-fried mountain greens with mushrooms, potatoes with squash, and rice with red adzuki beans. It was also true that without his contacts and his way of doing business her yoga business would not be what it was much less be in existence.

"What about individual integrity?" she asked. "It's not right to cheat people."

"Who was cheated at the gate? What is the value of 'individual integrity' when weighed against what a whole group of people stands to gain? The guards at the gate benefited. Our hostess benefits from our visit, and we benefit. It's a win-win situation, as you Americans like to say."

"Law-abiding people—honest guards and people who make reservations in advance and people who pay the normal toll—they're not benefiting. There's so much corruption in China. The news is censored here, but what we don't see in the Chinese media is that there are mass protests in the Chinese countryside and people are being imprisoned or even killed. These people are protesting because local officials are taking advantage of powerless villagers, and there's nothing they can do about any of it. They're losing everything they have and are becoming poorer while a few fat cats in the government and their cronies become obscenely wealthy. It's corrupt and wrong."

"Our media may leave some things out. Things that would not be beneficial for people to know." Malcolm chopsticked up a piece of fish and chewed thoughtfully. "I think this is the kind of scenario you are talking about," he continued. "Poor peasants in the Anhui countryside lost land for farming because a Shanghai-based company bribed local officials to free up land so it could build a large manufacturing facility. They also bribed EPA officials so they could side-step environmental regulations that prohibit the use of the chemicals they use in the manufacturing of their product—chemicals that are banned in the US and in Europe but are still sold to Chinese companies. So, the local officials have become richer, the EPA officials have become richer and the Shanghai company owners have become richer. Also, the owner's extended family benefits. The workers from the countryside have work they would not have otherwise." He paused. "Are you following me so far?" Natalie nodded warily as Malcolm helped himself to some greens.

"The Americans who commissioned and buy this company's product benefit from not paying the higher prices they would otherwise need to pay because American workers would never work for as long or as little as the poor Chinese worker in the countryside who has lost his land. Also," he continued thoughtfully, "American air, soil and water are not polluted by the waste products generated in the manufacturing process."

Natalie looked at Malcolm hard for a second then looked down at her bowl. She had never suspected that the easy-going, always joshing, rather paternalistic Malcolm she had known until now was actually aware of and thought about such things. "No one is benefiting, really, even if a few people are getting richer," she said.

Malcolm nodded but gave a small shrug. "It's the price we pay to develop and modernize our country," he said.

"What you're saying is that I shouldn't say anything about the way things are done here in China because I, as an American, benefit from what happens here—the corruption, the exploitation of poor peasants, the environment being destroyed, everything."

"What I'm saying," he replied patiently, "is that people are just living their lives in the best way they can given the choices available to them. Our country has made enormous progress in a very short amount of time. Millions have been lifted out of poverty these past couple of decades and are enjoying lives of abundance and security. All things considered, I would say we're something of a success story.

"I understand democratic ideals and yes, they're good ideas...in theory and for a population of a limited size," he said. He stared at the table for a long moment, his chopsticks balanced loosely in the hand he rested against the table edge.

"Listen, my friend," he said in a tone she had never heard before. Though he had already been speaking softly, he lowered his voice even further. "Where do you think I was during the June Fourth Democracy movement in Tiān'ānmén Square?" In 1989 she had been eight years old and a third grader in Mrs. Johnson's class. Suddenly she realized how much older he was.

"Sixteen years ago...were you studying at Tsinghua University at that time?"

"I was an idealistic university student, and I joined the mass demonstrations for democracy in Tiān'ānmén Square." Malcolm let this new bit of information sink in. "I was there. I saw what happened when our government sent in tanks and soldiers to disperse the thousands who had gathered.

"The soldiers started firing at the crowds to get them to move, but there were so many people there was nowhere for them to go. We were only students. I was never so scared in my life. I don't know if you've ever been in a crowd of that size, but everyone panicked and it was complete chaos. Those in the front couldn't go anywhere. They fell like *duōmǐnuò*, like dominoes."

Natalie thought about the iconic image of the man who had stood up to the tanks that rolled into Tiān'ānmén Square that day. She imagined a younger Malcolm there to witness the government opening fire on its own people. Hundreds, possibly thousands of peaceful protesters were gunned down that day.

"What can people do when faced with tanks and guns? We understand and accept that the government will do what it needs to do to keep the peace. It must protect society's interests, so what the Party says is law.

"But there is also what I call the people's law which has always been the real law regardless of what the government says. The government does what it does, and people do what they need to do. Everyone is just doing what he needs to do. For some, it's a matter of day-to-day survival, and for others it's still survival but of a different kind. In the end it's all about survival." Malcolm's glance swept the courtyard again, still casual, but he appeared to be assessing the other diners. No one was paying them any attention, but when he continued he had lowered his voice so much that Natalie had to lean towards him to hear.

"I speak frankly with you, *Nàtǎlì*, because you're an American. My Chinese friends and I don't talk about our experiences though we all know what we've seen and lived through. I abide by the Party's laws which help to keep the peace, but I also work according to the people's law. The June Fourth incident taught me, as it taught many who were there, that some activities are allowed and condoned in our society, and some are not. If one is wise one avoids engaging in questionable activities. It's best to not draw attention to oneself."

Malcolm said nothing for a long time as he studied her face.

"At the same time, we all do what we need to do to survive and take care of our families. I'll give you an example of how the two laws work in my life. My sister has two children, both daughters. As you know, urban couples are only allowed one child in China. I won't bore you with the details, but let's just say it takes a lot of resources to raise a child who does not exist in the eyes of the government: there's schooling, health care, residency issues, fines. My mother asked me to help my sister's family, and I agreed in part because when we were young my older sister didn't finish her schooling so that I could. My family could only afford to support one child through school. I was younger, but I was the boy.

"I am very fond of my nieces and cannot imagine life without them. It is my duty—and I am absolutely willing—to work hard to support my aging mother and my nieces. I did not write either the Party's laws or the people's laws, but I do know my way around both. Frankly, I am satisfied with my life and am proud to be Chinese. No system is perfect—there will always be benefits and drawbacks to any system anywhere you live—but I would never want to live as you Americans do because from where I stand, I don't see that your way of life is a more attractive alternative to what I already have."

Natalie was quiet for a long time. "It's not about being Chinese or American, is it?" she said quietly. It was about the luck of the draw and where one happened to be born. She easily could have been sitting in Malcolm's place while he passed moral judgment on her. As things were, countless unknown forces had conspired to bring them together to this place and time so they could share a meal together and meet across the oceans that separated them. What were the odds?

"Truce?" Malcolm replied with a wink. "Though you and I are not at war!" She could feel his gaze on her for a long time even after she had looked down.

After dinner, Malcolm sauntered off to explore the village while she washed up in the closet-sized shower room beside the kitchen. All trace of the seriousness that had surfaced during their meal was gone, and Malcolm was back to his ultra-casual, easily amused self—the Malcolm she knew. Feeling suddenly tired and still cold, Natalie washed up quickly and found her way back to their room. She shivered out of her clothes and climbed onto the *kàng*, cocooning herself in one of the comforters, intentionally leaving the frumpy floral one for Malcolm. As she waited for him to return, she felt the countryside's inscrutable silence descend over her as palpably as a thick quilt wrapped around her head. Her ears rang with the lack of sound so that she was straining to hear nothing at all. The gentle sigh of her own breath and the dull thud of her heart were too small, too soft to fend off the stillness that absorbed everything into itself like the thick fog that descended over the Bay Area back home. She shifted the bedding a little to break the monotony of the silence, but the small sound of fabric rustling against fabric was quickly swallowed up by a huge nothingness. She felt very alone. Although she knew that the room was a part of a larger compound and that other guests were sleeping nearby, the thick, solid old walls allowed no sounds through whatsoever. She closed her eyes and hoped Malcolm would return soon. The loneliness was all but unbearable.

Cradled in the gentle warmth of the *kàng*, Natalie must have dozed off because the next thing she knew was Malcolm climbing onto the *kàng* next to her in the dark. He had turned off the fluorescent light, and the room was lit dimly by moonlight shining obscurely through the paper-covered lattice windows.

"It's so quiet here," she whispered.

"You're still awake."

"It's so still it feels like we're the only people alive."

"Does it scare you?"

She could hear a hint of amusement even in his whisper. "Of

course not," she said, but she was not being truthful. After a few moments, he rolled closer to her in the dark. He was so close she could smell his cologne and feel the heat of his body. When he slowly began to stroke her hair, she closed her eyes in the dark and did not stop him.

She also did not stop him when his hands found her breasts beneath her t-shirt. Then he leaned over and bit her gently on the neck. It was a controlled bite that communicated volumes. Fully awake now and her whole body charged, Natalie breathlessly considered the possibilities. She held the bedding open for him to enter.

When she heard the crinkle of plastic foil wrap being torn open, Natalie noted with surprise that Malcolm had come to Cuàndǐxia prepared. She did not have time to dwell on the realization, however, because he was already entering her quickly, almost forcefully.

It had been a long time for her, and she had not had many lovers in her life. The initial excitement soon gave way to a muted panic. As his body moved against hers, a dull pain began in Natalie's groin and spread upwards into her chest, filling her throat.

Malcolm was a confident, powerful lover. He maneuvered her into different positions, turning her onto her side then bringing her onto her knees. The more he moved against her, inside her, chafing the ache deep within, the more she could only think about staunching the hurt that was spreading through her body like spilled blood.

He came quickly and rolled off of her.

As Natalie listened to Malcolm's breath becoming even again beside her ear, she realized they had not even kissed and that their coupling had hardly made an impression in the inscrutable silence.

"I don't know what is worse. Having nothing to show for all my hard work or being betrayed by people I trusted," the young woman says.

"I can understand that," Wú tells her. "It is very painful. Like so many people in my generation, I gave my all to what I thought was right, and then I felt utterly betrayed."

"I can't even imagine what you must have endured," the young woman says. "I have wondered what it was like for people to live through those times. My mother talks about how hard it was for her family when they fled the mainland."

"I wish I could speak as frankly as you do," Wú says, looking at the young woman with admiration. "It is different for you because you are an overseas Chinese and you are young. I have never told anyone what I am telling you because we Chinese do not revisit much less share past hurts. We think it is better to move on and leave what's in the past in the past, but I do not believe that is the right way. When things are left unspoken they are like wounds that have closed up on the outside but continue to fester beneath the surface. They will only bring us trouble later on."

"I have heard that you are a healer. I would like to learn how to heal people, but qigong is not the right practice for me."

Wú smiles. "If you want to be a healer, the first person you need to heal is yourself."

# Shīzi

Inner Mongolia, 1969

The minute I stepped outside our *ger*, the new dog bared his teeth at me, his yellow eyes following my every move. I now carried a heavy herding club with me whenever I left the *ger*, and my hold on the club tightened as I balanced Banhar's food bowl in my other hand.

Banhar, a female puppy, had been a gift from Bayaraa, the surly man from that first meeting in the school gymnasium. After that first disastrous encounter, I had only seen him in passing and primarily when we were at odds regarding official business, so his appearance the day after we returned from the hospital was a surprise. Feeling deeply mistrustful of all Mongolian men at that point, I had not been welcoming. He saw the deep frown on my face but dismounted anyway. Reaching into the front of his *deel*, he pulled out a small, squirming ball of black and orange fur with two small, folded triangles for ears. Handing the ball of fur to me, he had said simply, in heavily accented Mandarin, that if we fed her she would be loyal to us and protect us. He cantered off before I could reply.

When I emerged from the *ger* with the food bowl, Banhar jumped up from where she had been keeping a cautious distance from the new dog and ran over to me, her tail wagging her whole body in ecstatic puppy greeting. She remained alert even in her excitement, however, and maneuvered to keep the other dog within her line of vision.

For several days now, she had been harassed and on edge as a young female coming into heat for the first time, and our *ger* had become the epicenter of an earnest and chaotic mating ritual. Male dogs appeared out of nowhere to be close to her, and at one point I counted some thirty dogs in the vicinity, some of whom trailed gnawed-off tethers and broken chain links from their collars. The dog with the yellow eyes had proven himself to be the feistiest and most intractable of all the dogs. Collarless and chainless, he had arrived even before Banhar had begun to show signs of heat, and he challenged anyone—human or canine—who tried to approach her. No one knew where he had come from, but he defended his position with a ferocity that kept even the other instinct-crazed males at bay.

With his bright yellow eyes, alert, upright ears, thick, black-tipped fur and a dark ridge that ran down his back like a river of soot, he looked more wolf than dog. The Mongolians who saw him shook their heads in grudging admiration. *Chono*, wolf, they muttered under their breaths while keeping a safe distance. Wolves were often seen in the area, but we usually only knew of their proximity from their mournful, bone-chilling cries at night. He is missing the two yellow spots above his eyes that true Mongolian dogs have, the Mongolians told me. It is bad having a dog like that around, they added. He will attack the sheep.

Nothing we did could drive him off, however. The other more domesticated and less determined dogs we were able to keep away with thrown rocks and exasperated shouts. Even the skillful herders who could lasso the wildest stallions could not catch this dog with their *uurgas*. He skirted their nooses with ease and nimble grace as if it were child's play. So he stayed on.

I tried to ignore the dog's meaningful stare as I stooped to place Banhar's bowl on the ground, and something went very wrong. The dog did not even growl a warning before he was streaking for my throat with the intensity of a lightning bolt. Instinct acting faster than thought, my arm shot up to block the attack, and the dog sank his teeth into my arm. If it had not been early spring and if I had not been wearing a thick sheepskin-lined *deel*, I would have lost my left arm. As it was, the dog's teeth easily pierced the *deel's* thick sleeve, and I felt his fangs sink into my forearm. Too late, I realized my mistake: in bending over to place the bowl on the ground, I had compromised my superior upright position. The dog, sensing my vulnerability, had seized the opportunity.

An anger deeper than fear exploded in me. I screamed like a madwoman as I struck out with the club. The dog released his grip and lunged again, but the second and third times he attacked I was ready and managed to land solid blows on his head and back. Again and again the dog charged, coming from different angles. I crouched in readiness as he came at me, snarling with a ferocity that froze my insides, but I fought back. Shīfu's gōngfu training from so many years ago took over my movements as I spun and twisted away from the dog's snapping jaws. Once the training took over, he never managed to get more than a few mouthfuls of *deel* and sheepskin which he ripped off without hesitation. I heard the sound of fabric and hide tearing and saw with that strange, immediate clarity that comes with excitement that shreds of wool dangled from the corners of his mouth.

He was not a foolish dog who attacked senselessly, however. Just as suddenly as he had begun the attack, the wolf-dog pulled up just short of the club's striking distance and stood his ground, ears and tail high, lips curled back. We glared at each other for some time before I realized that I was baring my teeth and snarling as well. My body throbbed with the energy of the fight as we faced off for several long minutes. Then, his point made, the dog sat down slowly on his haunches and the snarl gradually disappeared from his lips though he kept a steely wolf-glare fixed on my face. We had come to a truce, and I had earned his respect.

Still breathing hard, I slowly lowered the club. I had never felt such visceral fury before, and the fury burned away the numbness I had been feeling for many weeks after our return from the hospital. Everything came into sharp focus at that moment: what had happened to us was beyond unjust. We had been manipulated, lied to, and forced to live the best years of our lives in a savage place. Though extolled as our country's hope and future, our loyalty and hard work were rewarded not with promotion or recognition but with banishment to a hostile frontier where we fought for self-respect and dignity among people who spat when they saw us. Getting hurt was a real and constant threat.

As the anger from the fight receded, a deep sadness welled up in me, bringing with it a dark despair that overtook me completely. The energy from the fight gone, I stood on the snow-covered ground as a very small and helpless young woman who had nothing but a club to fight off the demons that were taking over her heart.

Banhar had scrambled out of the way during the fight, but she returned to my side and to the battered metal basin I used as her food bowl and began to eat in big, hurried gulps. To my surprise, the new dog did not attempt to steal her food. He adhered to some sort of unspoken canine code of honor even though his ribs protruded from his sides. Like a gentleman, he waited a respectful distance away and approached to lick the empty bowl only after Banhar had finished eating. I did not think a dog could have so much self-control. Nevertheless, I kept my eyes on him as I stooped for the bowl and went back inside the *ger*. When I came back out with more meat scraps and watered-down rice, he eyed me and the bowl but waited until I was a good distance away. Then, curling his lips to make sure the other dogs stayed away, he bolted the food with wolf-haste before resuming a watchful position next to Banhar.

Throughout all this, the other males had been watching and waiting; one of them grew bold and approached Banhar. The wolf-dog, lips curled, growled a deep warning that the other male countered with hair-raising rumbles of his own. In a replay of what had happened dozens of times over the last few days, the two dogs faced off, hackles raised, fangs bared, snarling savagely. Normally, after a lot of noise and posturing, the other dogs backed down, intimidated by the yellow glare. This time, however, ears flat back on his head, the challenger attacked first. Banhar's beau responded with such passion that he took the other dog by surprise. The challenger was larger and better fed, but the wolf-dog had spirit and was a better fighter. What he lacked in size or weight he made up in skill and a sheer willingness to fight. Jaws snapping audibly, the two dogs threw themselves into what I was sure was a life-and-death struggle. Rearing up on their hind legs like stallions, they fought with an intensity that took my breath away.

Within minutes, however, the wolf-dog was standing triumphantly over the other dog who crouched low to the ground, his ears back and teeth bared, tail between his legs. After standing over the challenger for a full ten minutes, snarling the whole time, he finally let the other dog skulk away on his belly. Other dogs did not fare as well. Many were left with shredded ears and bleeding gashes on their flanks.

Having dispatched the latest challenger, the wolf-dog shook himself as if to shake off the fight and turned back to Banhar. His whole demeanor changed when he approached her. Tail wagging high with short, merry strokes, his wolfish face creased into what I could only describe as a dog's equivalent of a smile: he looked just like a man courting a woman. In spite of my own fight with him just moments before, and in spite of the heaviness that had descended over me, I laughed out loud as I watched him trying to ingratiate himself to Banhar while she curled her lips at him. I liked his scrappiness, dignity, and even the silliness and decided to keep feeding him so he would stay. I named him *Shīzi*, for he had the spirit of a fierce and proud lion.

As I picked up the metal pails for the morning milking, I heard before I saw the male student as he ran panting up to our *ger*. Bent over double, fists resting heavily on his thighs, it took him several moments to regain his breath before he could speak. He was incoherent in his excitement. The fear in his eyes extinguished the pleasure the dogs had brought me, and I was instantly transported back to that night several months earlier. "Come quickly!" he finally managed. Without waiting to hear more, I threw a shawl around my shoulders to cover the ripped *deel* and got ready to follow him. Xiǎomèi had been peeling vegetables at the low table by the stove, but she recoiled at the sight of the disheveled student. He avoided looking at her as he stood by the door waiting for me to get ready. Seeing the fear in her eyes, I hesitated for a fraction of a second before I ushered Banhar into the *ger*.

"I'll be back. Banhar will keep you company and the new dog will keep people away because she's inside," I told her.

"I'll be alright," she said quietly. In that moment my heart ached for my friend—for her pain, for her strength, and for her dignity. I shut the door carefully behind me.

My left arm throbbed from the bite wound as we ran as quickly as we could, sliding on the smooth leather soles of our boots across the icy patches on the path. It was awkward, running and sliding, running and sliding, so we were slow getting to the river's edge. Many had already arrived before us and were huddled in small, silent groups. As we drew closer, I saw the still form on the ground. Ice-lined eyelashes, parted blue lips, thick glasses askew. The sad expression. It was as if he had only closed his eyes to sleep and was having a bad dream, but his hair and clothes were heavy with river water and ice. They had found him half in half out of the river, as if he could not make up his mind whether to stay or leave. The deep Mongolian cold had made the decision for him.

I felt that I was drowning too. We had been so focused on supporting Xiǎomèi that we had little energy to spare for our Poet. We comforted him half-heartedly when he lost his appetite and started having nightmares that made him yell and thrash about on the rare nights he was able to sleep. When he started drinking hard alcohol every night and could not complete even the simplest tasks at work, we did not say anything although we knew that it was not at all like him to be so negligent.

We told him to not blame himself. It had not been his fault. They had been outnumbered and he could not have helped her even if he had tried, but I am sure Poet sensed the things we did not say: he had been a coward. He had abandoned Xiǎomèi to save himself.

What were his thoughts when he felt the river water closing over his head?

*I should have done more. I should have done more. I should have done more.* The words set the pace for my footsteps back to the *ger* as I wiped my eyes with a torn sleeve. As someone the others looked to for leadership, I felt responsible for his death. I should have reached out to him and tried harder to talk to him. We had been exiled together. If we had held together as a group instead of silently blaming him maybe he would still be alive.

But how could he let life go like that? Why couldn't he fight to hold on as we were all doing? We were all victims of the same sad circumstance. None of us could have predicted how harsh our lives would be once we left the city and our families behind.

How could he have been so weak, I thought even as the tears fell in a stream.

How could we have not seen that he had been holding on by a thread?

How were any of us equipped to face the brutal life of the Mongolian countryside?

I had witnessed quite a few deaths in my young life by then, but those deaths had been experienced through a thick, distorted lens as a Red Guard. Blinded by the indoctrination I received, I believed that the people we struggled against deserved their fates because they were our enemies. It was different with Poet. We had worked alongside each other, shared countless meals together, sang together, and recited poetry. Losing him was like losing a brother.

What had impressed us the most about Poet, in addition

to his quiet wisdom and good sense, was that he possessed an amazing memory. While we had all dutifully memorized and recited numerous texts in school, Poet told us that his mind retained pictures of what he saw so he was able to recall and recite every single book he had ever read, and he had read a lot in his short lifetime. At the beginning, we did not believe him and tested him by showing him pages out of books we had brought with us to see if he really could remember things as well as he said he could. He astonished us by reciting what he had seen back to us as if he were reading from the page itself. Not only was he able to recite every one of the Chairman's works in their entirety—from the most famous lines to the more obscure essays—but he could recite entire works by Marx and Engels, along with the works of many socialist thinkers we had heard about only in passing or did not know at all.

While Poet's ability to recite the Socialist canon was what saved him from persecution before he was sent down to the countryside, we quickly discovered that his true passion was for Chinese literature, especially poetry, and his knowledge of the classics was even more impressive than his knowledge of modern works. He knew thousands of poems, all the classics, plus most of the major commentaries on the classics. Considering the vastness of the classical Chinese canon that encompasses thousands of years of history and philosophy, Poet possessed an extraordinary wealth of knowledge.

At first, as someone trained to smash the Four Olds, I dismissed Poet's knowledge and love of Chinese literature though I was, of course, impressed with his encyclopedic memory. We had not been able to bring many books with us to the countryside, so having him in our midst was better than having a library. We spent countless cozy evenings in our *ger* or the boys' *ger* after the day's work was finished, with the girls sitting on a bed on one side and the boys sitting on the other side. We listened to his recitations, debated the finer points of Socialist thought, and sang our favorite songs together. The longer we lived in isolation far from the political ideology of Beijing, the more we came to appreciate the beauty and depth of all that he taught us about Chinese literature. His love of the texts came through so clearly that it made us appreciate them in a way that our schooling had never managed to do. Though earnest in his explanations of the finer points of scholarship, he was never pedantic or overbearing. He would have made an excellent university professor like both his parents, and his students would have held him in the highest regard.

Ice-lined lashes and blue lips.

All the texts he had stored in his head, the stories and philosophies he had introduced to us, gone. I could still hear his voice clearly in my head—that certain tone he adopted when he was talking about something he was passionate about.

I stopped outside our *ger*, mittened hand around the door pull. I did not know how to tell Xiǎomèi. I turned away and slumped down next to the corral. I do not know how long I sat there with my forehead against my knees, but after a while the bawling of the tethered calves together with the imperious trumpeting of the cows broke through my haze and reminded me that the morning's milking was still waiting for me. The bitter morning cold had seeped into the very marrow of my bones, and I knew I could not afford to stay still much longer, exposed as I was to the elements. The front of my *deel*, soaked with tears, was frozen solid.

I broke the ice across my chest and got to my feet with a deep sigh. Life in the countryside continued as it always did, indifferent to human loss. Unless I wanted to become one of the dead myself, I needed to move on and attend to the living.

# Cold Water

BEIJING, 2005

MASTER ZHU SURPRISED NATALIE by opening the door before she had had time to ring the doorbell. He was talking on his cell phone, but his smile was warm as he stepped aside to let her pass. She was almost across the threshold when, out of the corner of her eye, she caught sight of a security camera mounted above her head. She felt relieved and smiled at her own apprehension: so that was how he had been able to anticipate her arrival. It wasn't the psychic x-ray vision he had demonstrated on her first visit though one never knew what a qigong master could or could not do.

Master Zhu closed the heavy doors behind them and, holding his hand over the mouthpiece, he immediately excused himself—he would only be a few minutes.

Left alone in the courtyard that she remembered so well, Natalie relaxed a little in the serenity: the pond and the graceful willows, the immaculate gray flagstones, the cheerful, bright vermilion pillars. The surface of the expansive tree root table had been cleared of all tea-making implements and held a single white ceramic bowl filled with small, pink tea roses. Natalie stooped to take in the faint fragrance of the blossoms, running her hand across the polished tabletop that recalled the rich hue of brewed tea. She wondered who in Master Zhu's household was responsible for the flowers. It was a nice, feminine touch.

When Master Zhu still had not returned after several minutes, Natalie dropped into a squat beside the pond to watch the fat koi fish gliding about beneath the lily pads. Post-Cuàndǐxia, things would be different now between her and Malcolm. Was it bad to sleep with one's business partner and housemate? He was away on business most of the time, but what could they lose in exploring the relationship?

Several cupped handfuls of very cold water landed on Natalie's back, and she lurched back from the pond's edge. She scrambled to her feet to face Master Zhu who, face creased into a wide Cheshire cat grin, was carefully wiping his hands on the front of his trousers.

"You are too much in your head. It's an affliction," he said. "Most people these days are too hot, too heady, too yang. You needed the cool, moistening yin properties of the water." It was a warm day for October, but it was not so warm that Natalie appreciated being doused with smelly green pond water. Master Zhu's grin was so wide, however, that she smiled a little too.

"Come inside. Drink some tea," he said simply as if nothing out of the ordinary had happened.

In a small room that adjoined the courtyard, thick wool rugs woven in deep reds and mustard yellows covered the floor. Framed black and white portraits of old, stern, qigong masters hung from the three inner walls of the room. The fourth wall, made up of sliding wooden panels, opened onto the courtyard. The maze-like patterns of the lattice windows were similar to the windows of the courtyard home where she and Malcolm had stayed the night before, but here the lattice was backed with glass, not brittle paper. The fall sunshine, hazy with smog, shone gently into the room. There was no furniture, a low table aside, and they sat on the floor on satin meditation cushions. Master Zhu settled easily into a lotus position, but Natalie could only get into half lotus, favoring her right knee. In the weeks that had passed since her first visit and the unexpected healing, she had noticed less pain in the knee but it was still there, phantom-like, lurking in the background of her daily movements and yoga practice. Her yoga top, still damp, clung uncomfortably to her back and shoulders.

"I have studied with many grandmasters and each one taught me invaluable things," Master Zhu said, nodding toward the unsmiling faces on the walls. "What I realized, however, was that the old traditions do not address the specific problems that modern humans face. People have practiced qigong for thousands of years, but the old forms developed under very different conditions in very different times. Back then, dedicated practitioners had the luxury of practicing for hours on end for days, months at a time. People could devote an entire lifetime to perfecting a single technique.

"We have made so much progress as a species! Our pace of life is hundreds of times faster than our ancestors'. We can accomplish so much more and more efficiently, so modern people need modern tools. Our fast-paced life demands that we use accelerated healing techniques. For the past twenty years, I have been teaching people how the practice of qigong can be accelerated too." Master Zhu surveyed the portraits on the walls then turned away from them.

"You are wondering how one can modernize qigong," he said, as if reading Natalie's mind, reminding her that she needed to guard her very thoughts with someone like Master Zhu. "This is your first lesson. There is no need for us to dwell too much on the basics which I think you are already familiar with through your readings. Plus, you practice yoga," he added generously, all trace of the antagonism she had sensed during their first meeting gone. "It's very simple, really. We restore what's been lost in people's lives, and we use tools that are faster than anything that has come before."

Master Zhu's system, called Ascendant Yin Gong, was premised on the idea that the female or yin element on earth had been suppressed for too long, and large-scale oppression and misunderstanding of the feminine were the causes of most problems in the world. The imperialistic West was very yang: active, hot, masculine, individualistic, ambitious and exploitive. The East traditionally had been more yin: yielding, passive, group-oriented and expansive. Modern Chinese people, as a result of Western influences, had become overly yang which resulted in numerous yang-type ailments: high blood pressure, heart disease, inflammatory diseases, migraines, ulcers, digestive disorders...the list went on and on. To counteract the overabundance of yang energy that was the root cause of most people's health problems, Master Zhu's new qigong techniques emphasized cultivation of yin energy to balance the excessive yang in people's lives.

"That is why you needed a bit of cold water," Master Zhu said with a glimmer of that Cheshire cat grin. "It was cold and wet, and it was very effective in getting you out of an excessively yang state." Natalie's clothes had not dried yet, and she was starting to feel a little chilled as she sat still for Master Zhu's lecture.

"If one balances and nurtures the yin, then naturally the yang comes into balance as well." The qigong master's voice took on an oratorical quality as he explained the specifics of Ascendant Yin Gong. There were three main branches. Each branch consisted of four sub-practices, and each sub-practice was associated with five specific movements or meditations. "Three branches, four practices, and five movements," he told her. It sounded simple enough, but Master Zhu's practice consisted of no less than sixty elements. He had lost her on the third sub-practice of the second branch, or was it the fourth movement of the third sub-practice of the third branch?

As Master Zhu continued to expound on his qigong system, his voice took on the timbre and cadence of Chinese bureaucrats when they delivered official speeches on CCTV, the government mouthpiece. It was the same way the pastor at her mother's fundamentalist Chinese church in San Francisco delivered his sermons week after week, year after year. She had dutifully accompanied her mother to church for as long as she had lived at home, but then, as now, her immediate reaction was to tune out.

The Chinese had a penchant for organizing things into pithy threes, fours and fives. Natalie had felt similarly overwhelmed when confronted with the Communist Chinese timeline in a modern Chinese history course in college: the Three Antis Campaign; the Five Antis Campaign; the Three Freedoms and One Contract Campaign; the One Attack and Three Antis Campaign; the Four Cleansings Campaign; the Smash the Four Olds Campaign. Most Chinese, drilled for years in rote memorization, had excellent memories for dates, facts and figures. Natalie, a product of the American educational system, found that she could only hold about three pieces of information in her head at any given time. As Master Zhu droned on about the various branches and sub-branches, she was soon completely lost.

Despite an inability to fully grasp the intricacies of all that he was telling her, Natalie could not help feeling a little dubious about his system. There were contradictions in his theory, for one. As the "modernizer" of an ancient system of healing, Master Zhu wanted to speed things up, yet wasn't the impatient pace of modern life largely to blame for many modern ailments? His brand of healing sounded almost like a fast-acting product that could be worked into a busy lifestyle. Moreover, he claimed that suppression of the feminine element was to blame for most of the world's problems, but his own teaching style was thoroughly paternalistic. Despite what he said about restoring and cultivating the gentle, intuitive feminine, he readily assumed the role of an older male authority figure while she, the younger female, was expected to listen quietly without interruption or discussion.

Natalie blinked back to attention when she realized he had stopped speaking and was observing her closely. "You are not feeling well," he said. He was right: her abdomen felt clenched and knotted, as if something she had eaten did not agree with her. She had noticed the cramping when she awoke that morning on the large *kàng* in Cuàndǐxia, but then she and Malcolm were getting ready for breakfast and were off to explore the village. Malcolm had looped his arm around her waist as they walked, and he had pressed her up against the cold stone walls of the narrow alleyways for kisses, his hands finding her breasts beneath her shirt. Returning his kisses between the laughter, she had prayed that other tourists would not come wandering by and see them. They had taken photos of each other in front of the village temple where people used to pay respects to various gods and ancestors, and then they had sneaked more kisses inside the temple when they found themselves alone. Giggling and pushing him away, she had had to stop him from all but making love to her on the temple's now-empty altar.

So she had ignored the pain. Now that she had been sitting still for a while, however, the cramping had become so intense that it was difficult for her to sit upright. She wondered what Master Zhu, with his uncanny ability to read energy fields, was able to see in her. Did he detect her skepticism about his teachings? Could he sense the changes in her life as of last night? She felt very exposed. The pain in her belly was getting worse.

"Close your eyes," Master Zhu said, his tone suddenly and unexpectedly very gentle. The pain was so acute that it was all Natalie could do to not double over. She heard him get up to kneel behind her, and then she felt one of his hands at the base of her spine and the other one between her shoulder blades. His touch was light, and heat from his palms radiated soothingly through the damp fabric of her top.

It was only when the qigong master placed his hands on her back that Natalie realized how balled up her body was, like a tight fist. She gasped as pain of an intensity she had never felt before flooded her.

"Keep your eyes closed," he said firmly.

Natalie closed her eyes again. Arms braced in front of her crossed legs to keep herself from falling forward, she tried to breathe more slowly even as she felt herself beginning to panic.

Dimly, from within the tenderness of her body, she saw a blue-gray cat with a long, curving tail and gold-specked green eyes.

The cat hissed at Natalie from the tight space beneath a chest of drawers where only her eyes, a deep, refractive green in the darkness, were visible. Ten-year-old Natalie reached a hand under the bureau and received a lightning-fast swat from a bandaged paw and a hard bite that drew blood. She pulled her hand back in a hurry. Her mother would be home soon. Leaving the cat underneath the bureau, she quickly gathered up rags and cleaning supplies and went downstairs to work in the corner of her mother's once immaculate living room. Once or twice she looked up quickly, guiltily, thinking she heard the garage door opening, but it was only the air conditioning starting up or a car passing by outside. After a few minutes, she sat back on her heels to survey the carpet but saw that there was still a huge, telltale yellow stain where she had been working. The unmistakable stench of cat urine persisted beneath the chemically smell of the cleaner. Natalie looked around the room. Her mother's prized plants drooped sadly from kitten-chewed stems, and black soil littered the white carpet around the planters. The small crystal figurines and delicate blown-glass art pieces that had lined the mantelpiece—pricey mementos of her father's reconciliation attempts that had taken them to Europe, South America and Asia—had long since been taken down and stored beyond the reach of mischievous paws. The corners of the tan leather couches were pierced with hundreds of tiny claw marks, and tattered silk tassels hung sadly from hand-embroidered silk cushions, their faces a mess of broken threads.

The kitten had been a gift from Natalie's father. Natalie saw him only once or twice a year after he moved back to Taiwan. On one of his rare visits home before the divorce was finalized, he had silently handed Natalie the round ball of gray fur. Seeing her immediate delight, a ghost of a smile had appeared in the corners of his eyes before he had turned to face Natalie's mother. *Who's going to take care of it,* her mother had demanded, her voice rising. *The girl is young and irresponsible. I don't want to have an animal in the house.*

Clutching the kitten tightly to her chest, Natalie had escaped to her room in the ensuing battle.

"What are you doing?" Natalie's mother stood in the doorway. Natalie looked up at her and could not say anything. Even if the cleaning supplies had not been scattered around her, her face gave everything away. Her mother's lips tightened as she turned away without a word. It would have been easier if she had said something, but there was nothing she could do faced with her mother's silence.

Natalie dropped the cleaning rag and sprinted upstairs but heard outraged yowling before she could get to her mother's bedroom. Natalie's mother had dragged the kitten out from under the bureau by its hind legs and was shoving it into the cat carrier. Bandaged front paws scrabbled uselessly against the carpet.

Natalie had always been silent while her parents battled it out. Unable to help, too scared to take sides, it was better that she remained forgotten. After her father left for good to be with the other woman, Natalie's mother focused all her attention on Natalie: her grades were too low; she was lazy; the money spent on her piano lessons was a waste since she never practiced enough; she was as lanky and awkward as a bamboo pole—in a word, unattractive. Even her face with its big nose was an affront, as she was the spitting image of her father. When friends came by for tea, mahjong and gossip, Natalie's mother complained about her daughter openly, not caring that she was in the room to hear.

It was a surprise, then, even to herself when she launched into her mother with all the fury that her ten-year-old body could muster. "It's your fault," she screamed, lunging for the cat carrier. "*You* did this to her! She can't use the litter box because you mutilated her. You never wanted her in the first place. She's the one thing I love and you have ruined her. Now you are taking her away. *I hate you!*" Natalie's mother wrestled the carrier away from her daughter and started for the stairs, her jaw set. Natalie ran to her room, slammed the door as hard as she could, and threw herself face down onto the bed. She hated seeing the pain in her mother's face.

Dark gray fur and luminous, gold-flecked green eyes filled Natalie until she was crying with great, heaving sobs. A powerless ten-year-old girl once again, she missed the kitten's purr that had filled her chest when they snuggled together in bed.

She missed her father.

Deep despair, the floodwaters of loss, surged through her sweeping away the hundreds of carefully constructed dikes she had erected every time she assured herself that she was alright, she was fine. Now a great dam had broken open and wave after wave of grief flooded her, filling every crevice and fissure of what had been, for a very long time, a well-guarded and barren flood plain.

Natalie cried for a long time. She cried until she was senseless. When she finally came to, she realized that Master Zhu had placed a fresh pot of tea on the table in front of her. The master himself was nowhere to be seen. Carefully, trying to steady her shaking hands, she poured herself a cup only to realize that the pot had already cooled.

Exhausted and empty, she sipped the tea slowly. Then she felt the sunlight, warm on her skin, as it shone gently through the lattice-framed windows. In the space that the tears had washed clear, she realized that the inner flood plain, clean and bare, sparkled a little in that sunlight. She savored the sun's warmth on her skin, the fragrant and slightly bitter tea, the quiet of the space.

Someone was in the room. Turning quickly, she saw that Xiǎo Gāng had come in so quietly that she had not noticed. He sat a distance away from her on one of the round meditation cushions and his face shone with tears. In his hand he held a small bouquet of pink tea roses that he extended towards her, his face averted. Taking the roses slowly from his large hands, Natalie felt herself tearing up again. It was not just the sunlight shining on his hulking figure that made the room so warmly luminous.

Natalie brought the flowers up to her face, closed her eyes, and took a deep breath. The ten-year-old girl and the kitten were of the past. She was an adult now, and regardless of what was in store for her and Malcolm, she could look forward to the relationship as it unfolded. Everything would be fine.

Relaxing into the newfound sense of peace, she felt an abrupt lack of warmth, as when a cloud moves in front of the sun. She opened her eyes just in time to see Xiǎo Gāng leaving in a hurry, throwing glances over his shoulder at his father who had stepped aside to let him pass.

*"How do I heal myself?"* the young woman asks.

*Wú smiles at her question. "If you're asking this question then you've already begun. You start where you are. You ask your heart what hurts are hiding inside it. It will tell you." Wú picks up her market basket which she had set down next to the door. "Come, I was just about to go to the market. We can chat as we walk."*

# Shīfu Visits



I stood among the remains of what had been my *ger* in the bleak morning light, my feet covered in hot ashes. Around me, like the bars of a birdcage, the *ger's* burnt frame loomed over the blackened innards of the meager life I had tried to carve out for myself in the countryside. The heavy wooden bed was only partially burnt, but my bedding was a charred mess. There was no place for me to sleep.

As the flames had shot into the sky in the pre-dawn gloom, I had watched in horror and fascination as all that I owned was reduced to ashes. Now that the fire had died down, I felt only the wind, my constant companion, as indifferent as it was chilling. Feeling dead inside, I could not muster a single tear to wet my dry eyes.

I knelt among the ashes in a daze. When I finally looked up, my soul just about jumped out of my body, for standing in front of me was Shīfu as if he had not died at our hands almost three years ago. I blinked, looked hard, and blinked again. Was this a vision? Was he a ghost come back from the dead? I began to sweat profusely despite the bitter cold until I saw that his face was serene and kindly.

*Do you have an answer to the question?*

I had an abundance of questions. I had lost my friends and lost faith in the Party's omnipotence. More questions were forming all the time, but I immediately understood which question he meant. "I don't have time to practice qigong in the countryside," I said, not daring to look into the master's eyes. "We've struggled just to survive these past few months. My *ger* has burned down. I don't have anything left." I knew even as I spoke that I was making excuses and felt as ashamed as the adolescent who had been sent away by the master so many years ago.

*What* do *you have?*

I looked around me at the smoking ruins. "My dogs were outside—they were spared. Their barking woke me up."

*What else do you have?*

I sighed deeply. "I have nothing left."

*What do you need to learn?* He was so calm, so full of authority, that nothing but a considered answer would do. There is a lesson in every trial, he had told his students. Nonetheless, I could not help regretting the fact that even the small amount of money I had sewn into my bedding was gone. With my very survival so precarious, where would I find the heart to practice qigong, and what good would it do me? I did not have an answer to Shīfu's questions.

Shīfu kept looking at me. He looked so long and so steadily that something within me broke. I wept out of self-pity and weakness. Things had come to an end for me in the countryside, and I did not have the strength to start over.

My hands clasped tightly over my chest, I awoke in a sweat, the corners of my eyes moist from crying in my sleep. I let out a long sigh when a quick glance around the *ger* confirmed that our home had not burned down in the middle of the night. All was as usual: the three beds were neatly made, the same three dusty, faded red carpets covered the grass that our summer *ger* rested over, and the washed ceramic bowls and chopsticks were stacked neatly on a towel on the low table ready for our evening meal. All was fine, untouched by flames.

Things were not the same, however. The bed Xiǎomèi had slept in was neatly made up like the others but there was a stillness about it that belied the fact that it had been many weeks since anyone had lain on it. On too many nights to count before we finally obtained permission for her to return to Beijing, I had woken in the middle of the night first to her muffled sobs and then to her sweat-soaked body crawling into bed next to me. On such nights I held her gently, stroked her hair, and sang softly to her. We fell asleep that way but were often awakened again by more nightmares.

Taking the metal ladle from its usual place next to the door, I filled the kettle using the water that we hauled, bucket by laborious bucket, from the river where Poet had died. I still found myself coming up with questions I wanted to ask him only to remember, an instant later, that he was gone. I placed the kettle on the stove that we had moved outside for the summer and let out a long sigh as I waited for the tea water to boil.

As the kettle began to hiss and rock on its uneven base, I went inside the *ger* to retrieve Xiǎomèi's latest letter from beneath my pillow. Sitting down on a low stool just outside the open doorway, I rested my elbows on my knees and looked out over the steppes, the envelope dangling loosely from my hand. There was no need to remove the single sheet of paper to read the handful of penned lines I already knew by heart.

The summer landscape before me was a very familiar sight by then: the sweeping grassland dotted with the round white tops of distant *gers*, the small pale specks of livestock like grains of rice strewn across a thick green rug, and rolling hills to the east that glowed a deep coral red with the sunset. Soon it would be time to pen up the animals, and the trumpet-like calls of the cows coming in for the evening milking confirmed that I had slept for a long time. I tucked Xiǎomèi's letter into the front flap of my *deel* and drank some tea. Rubbing the heels of my hands briskly over my eyes and face, I smoothed away the wrinkles of uneasy sleep and melancholy thoughts before I joined the other women for the evening milking.

The men had begun corralling the sheep and goats, and the cows, udders bursting, were sauntering in in small family groups.

A smart, feisty sorrel, my favorite, mooed pointedly at me as she nosed her calf through the bars of the holding pen. I released the calf and watched his easy, simple joy in being reunited with his mother. I envied him as he suckled noisily, head compulsively butting her udder, tail swinging gleefully. After a few moments when the milk was flowing freely, I stuck two fingers into the calf's mouth for him to suck on and drew him away to be tethered. I then assumed a position that had become second nature to me after so many months: sitting on a low stool with my knees holding the bucket in place, I rested my forehead against the sorrel's warm flank. My fingers found the teats and I began to milk by touch, my scholar's hands and arms now as strong and calloused from rough work as a peasant woman's. It had been months since I had picked up a calligraphy brush.

Lost in the rhythmic ping-pinging sound of milk cascading into the bucket, I did not hear a rider come up to where we were milking until he was almost next to me. I looked up just in time to see him dismount. It was Bayaraa, the Mongolian man who had been so uncooperative at our first production meeting. Subsequent meetings had proven my intuition correct because he did indeed come from a well-respected herding family in the community and people listened to him. While the town had yet to make much progress with the production goals, our relationship with him, at least, had come a long way from that disappointing first encounter in which he had brusquely put me in my place.

After the first meeting, we still disagreed on a regular basis, but as I experienced the changing of the seasons in the countryside and personally witnessed the delicate balance between humans, animals and Nature that he had spoken about, I began to understand that we had been sent to the countryside on a fool's errand. I argued my points with less and less conviction but was reluctant to concede that he had been right all along. Bayaraa, on his part, seemed less interested in being right than in showing us that not all Mongolians were hateful or to be feared. Perhaps he felt remorse for what his fellow townsmen had done because after our return from the hospital he made a point of dropping by from time to time to check up on us and to lend a hand. He was never overly friendly nor did he ever have much to say, but he never hesitated to assist the remaining male student in his work or to teach us the skills we needed to survive in the countryside. From learning how to batten down our *gers* during windstorms, to handling the animals in a way that would keep both us and the animals safe, to making yogurt, cheese, dried curds, and the dozens of other dairy products that make up the Mongolian diet, there was so much we needed to learn that first year. Bayaraa was a patient teacher even for tasks that were traditionally performed by women, and having him as an ally proved to be a great blessing. Not only did he help us survive that first year, but his generosity bolstered our relationship with the locals because the townspeople respected him.

Though highly protective of us and mistrustful of visitors, Banhar and Shīzi barked a few times in warning but then greeted Bayaraa enthusiastically as he came over to where I was milking. He stood for a moment to let the dogs sniff his *deel* and boots. "I was at the post office. This came for you," he said, pulling a letter from the front of his *deel*. It had been several weeks since Xiǎomèi last wrote. Wondering if she received my short missives—I wrote three letters for every one I received from her—I stowed the thin envelope next to the other one in the front of my *deel* to read later.

"We are almost finished here," I said to him. "Why don't you join us for dinner?" The original group from Beijing had already been small, but now with both Xiǎomèi and Poet gone, the three of us who remained felt like the fragments of a broken bowl. We welcomed Bayaraa's company whenever he stopped by and always urged him to stay for the evening. It did not take us long to discover that though he said little, Bayaraa had a beautiful singing voice. One of the few pleasures for us at that time was when the four of us spent cozy evenings in the *ger* while Bayaraa sang and taught us Mongolian songs. His resonant baritone, honed from years of serenading horses out on the wide-open grassland, filled the *ger* and our hearts.

The evening meal was simple because we did not have access to the spices and vegetables one found in abundance in the city or even in the larger towns. As Bayaraa helped the male student finish securing the animals for the night, the other girl and I made noodles by slicing up several large, flat disks of dough we had oiled, rolled up and steamed. Noodles of all shapes and sizes were easily purchased in the city, but we made everything by hand in the countryside. The simplicity of country food had been a shock to us when we first arrived, but we soon grew accustomed to plain fare and even appreciated how good it could taste when eaten outdoors or in our *ger* after a long day of working in the sun, wind and snow. Even so, we still craved the dishes we could only get in Beijing, and some of our most animated conversations were about the foods we missed the most.

"Mongolian food is much indebted to Chinese cuisine," I remarked when the four of us were seated around the low table. "These fried noodles, *tsuivan*, are basically *chǎomiàn*. Tsuivan, chǎomiàn... you got this dish from the Chinese."

"Your favorite meal of *buuz*," the other girl chimed in, "is just a cruder version of our *bāozi*. And you call tea *tsai*, which is from our word *chá*." The other girl and I enjoyed teasing Bayaraa because of his overly serious nature. He smiled so rarely that the more we got to know him, the more we teased him. We were rewarded with half of a smile though Bayaraa kept his attention on the contents of his bowl. "Come now," the other girl continued, "you people never even used bowls or chopsticks before you encountered the Chinese. You still eat with your hands and use knives at the table."

"Which is why," I finished for her, "we always considered you to be barbarians."

"Their traditional way of life was one of survival," the boy said when Bayaraa said nothing and continued to eat at a leisurely pace. "The climate and terrain are not suited to the comforts that come with agrarian settlement."

When he finished eating, Bayaraa picked up the kettle and filled his bowl with tea which we had prepared the Chinese way, without milk. "He's right," he said after he had taken a few long, loud sips from his bowl. Tiny drops of oil from the *tsuivan* floated on the surface of his tea. I got up to rinse and wipe my bowl clean before I filled it with tea. The other students did the same, tossing the rinse water out the open door onto the grass outside. Although the only tea we could get in the countryside was of the poorest grade—low quality leaves pressed with stems and sticks into large bricks that we shaved with our knives—we still preferred it unadulterated in any way. The locals put milk and salt in their tea and sometimes even added butter for flavor.

"We eat meat in the wintertime and dairy products in the summertime," Bayaraa continued. "In the summertime, there are wild plants and berries, but otherwise we get everything we need from our animals. Our life may be simple compared to what you are used to, but it is the best way to live on this land." While our own small town was focused on improving animal husbandry practices, I knew that he was referring to development projects in other parts of the province in which locals were settled into communes and taught to till the land and raise pigs and chickens for meat and eggs. "The Han way of life is not right here. The land is not suited for cultivation. We move our animals constantly because the grass cannot sustain continuous grazing. There are so many Han people here now. We cannot stop the changes they are bringing with them."

Bayaraa spoke without bitterness or resentment—he simply stated what we all knew to be true—but his words hung heavily on us as we finished our tea in silence. As naïve participants of the

Han migration he spoke about, we were caught in the unenviable position of both colonizer and abandoned exile.

Even half a year before I would have argued that the traditional nomadic way of life was backwards: herders did not have access to running water or electricity much less know anything about basic sanitation. All these things were true, but now that we ourselves had lived this way for a while, it was not as dreadful as it had first seemed. Of course, I often found myself missing the comforts of urban life and wondered how much longer our reeducation would last or if we would ever be able to return to the city. Given the political climate at the time, however, it was by no means a certainty for any of us.

After dinner, perhaps to lighten the mood, Bayaraa reached into his *deel* and pulled out a small, worn brocade pouch. "These are a matched pair," he said as he tipped the bag over. Four small sheep ankle bones, oblong and scraped clean, spilled into his broad palm. "Two of these *shagai* are from a male sheep and the other two came from a female from the same flock. The two animals were slaughtered for a feast for an official visit. It was early in the winter when the sheep were at their fattest so it was a good time to slaughter them, but when the women cleaned the animals they found two tiny fetuses in the female's womb. It's very, very bad to kill a pregnant animal. We prayed to the animal's spirit and asked for forgiveness, then we wrapped the fetuses in fat and burned them as an offering to the spirits."

"Why did you keep the *shagai* if killing the animal was bad?" I asked.

Bayaraa's thick, rough fingers caressed the smooth bones as he considered the question. "For us to live, others must die. Our existence depends on the life and death of everything else in the world. Lives are given to support our existence. I have kept the *shagai* as a reminder of this," he replied. I looked at the wide, ruddy face across from mine, trying to reconcile Bayaraa's elegantly simple words with his bulky, broad-shouldered form. His weather-reddened cheeks were still smooth but bore testament to the countless days he spent with the horses out on the grassland in all weather and in all seasons. Uneducated though he was, he often surprised me with his good sense. Growing up in such a demanding environment required him to be both alert and intelligent, but the intelligence had more to do with animal survival and instinct than, for example, Poet's cultivated knowledge. The more time I spent with Bayaraa, the more I found myself respecting the man and the culture that he took such care to introduce to us.

"There are many games you can play with *shagai*, but most Mongolians use them for divination," he said. He turned the bones over to show us the distinct sides that represented the four most important animals for Mongolians. Of the two narrow sides, the smoother side had a graceful curve that looked like the profile of the most auspicious of the animals, the horse. Opposite the horse, a deep S-shaped groove represented the less auspicious camel. The broad side that was rounded and smooth represented the sheep which brought abundance and luck. The flip side, however, with its deep groove and horns represented the unlucky goat. "We ask the *shagai* questions and they give us answers. This set has always given me good advice." Cupping the *shagai* between his broad palms, Bayaraa blew into his hands before he tossed the bones onto a handkerchief he had spread on the table. They fell with a clatter. He studied the formation for a moment then looked up. "There will be enough rainfall this year and the animals will fatten up nicely before winter," he said. "It will be a good summer for the animals."

"Isn't it backwards and superstitious to believe that sheep ankle bones can tell us anything about the future?" I asked.

"There are many things we do not understand, but they are still true," he replied. "Why don't you ask the *shagai* a question?"

Curiosity getting the better of us, we took turns casting the bones while he read them for us. When it was my turn, I was still doubtful but wanted to see what the bones had to say: given a very rough first year, how would our lives in the countryside unfold in the coming year? The bones landed with one camel, one sheep, and two goats. Bayaraa studied them for such a long time that I grew uneasy. "Is it not auspicious?" I asked. He looked up at me.

"You must work hard," was all he would say.

After Bayaraa left that evening, leaving the *shagai* with us as a small gift, I was troubled by so many thoughts that I could not sleep. The rational side of me struggled with the idea of giving credence to something as arbitrary as a bone reading, but I could not help feeling a sense of foreboding. If the coming year's prospects had been favorable, Bayaraa would not have paused for such a long time before giving me his interpretation. He must have seen something in the bones that he was not telling me.

Bayaraa surprised us with his simple trust in *Tengger* the Sky Father, *Gazar Eej* the Earth Mother, and countless other spirits and supernatural forces. Everything had a spirit, and everything was worshipped: fire, wind and rain spirits, spirits of the hills and grasslands, river and lake spirits, spirits for all the different animals, and malevolent spirits that caused diseases and wreaked havoc in people's lives. If Han people were superstitious particularly when it came to ancestor worship, Mongolians, who lived their lives deeply connected to Nature, were many times more superstitious. They found meaning in rock formations, in weather patterns, in their animals' behavior, in almost anything that could be read. Things such as *shagai* answers or the itching of one's palms when a friend was about to arrive unannounced were taken as a matter of course. For the Mongolians, these signs were unfailingly accurate indicators of what was to come.

I was dismissive at first of the Mongolians' unsophisticated thinking, but it did not take many months of living as they did for me to see that our urban knowledge was all but useless for a life that was at the mercy of the elements. Despite the active role I had taken in smashing the feudal, superstitious past, the longer I lived in the countryside far from the protective walls of the city, the more I harbored deep, irrational fears: I became terrified of things I could not see, of forces beyond our control, and of spirits who could come into our lives unbidden and create trouble for us. Having now lived through the bitterly cold temperatures and snowstorms of winter and the violent windstorms of spring, I had never felt more helpless in the face of powerful, ruthless Nature or, as Bayaraa would say, mighty *Tengger's* will.

As I tossed and turned, I wondered if respect for the Mongolian gods and spirits could help one stay alive in the countryside since many of the folk beliefs had practical applications. The Mongolians were a much hardier people than we were and had survived for many millennia across thousands of miles of nomadic wanderings. They had lived through seasonal changes, droughts and *zuuds*, and they knew how to navigate the harsh terrain. Chinggis Khan, the fearsome conqueror of the Chinese and the much-revered father of the Mongols, was reputed to have been deeply in touch with the spirit world.

Even if Bayaraa had not introduced us to the *shagai* that evening, Shīfu's appearance in my dream that afternoon had left me shaken. I had felt his presence so strongly that it did not matter if I believed in ghosts or spirits. In the deep quiet of the night, I could no longer distract myself from the questions the dream had raised. What did I have left in this life? What was I supposed to learn from this experience in which the only constant was a feeling of uncertainty about the future? The *shagai* reading only deepened my apprehension at having reached a crossroads where the ideals I had built my life on had collapsed but I had nothing with which to replace the old paradigm.

Shīfu's death: the fall of a great bamboo amidst frenzied axes. For the first time since that fateful struggle session in which I had helped bring about his demise, I felt genuine and deep remorse. I had been a mindless ax, a tool wielded by those who used me for their own purposes before discarding me. Flooded with shame, I did not know if I could ever come to terms with what I had done, and I was only now, belatedly, beginning to understand the magnitude of the loss. What had become of his teachings? Where was the power he had embodied or the hope he had inspired in so many? His young son, a victim of circumstance like myself, had been a tender young shoot growing beside the master's fallen trunk, easily uprooted. Shīfu's students—few as they were—had scattered or gone underground in the climate of fear. Before all the madness, many had appeared on Shīfu's doorstep in need of his steady guidance and comfort. Where did people go for healing now?

When I was young, qigong practice had come naturally to me, and I had taken it for granted. Even the most challenging *gōngfu* forms that Shīfu taught his students had come easily to me after a few months of diligent practice. By the time Shīfu sent me away, I had felt as potent and powerful as a young tiger, but my efforts had lacked something. Many years later, unable to sleep in a Mongolian tent in the heart of the grassland, I finally understood that I had failed to progress because I had been too callow to understand the deeper principles that underpinned all that Shīfu taught his students. I had focused only on the physical movements and my practice had come from a place of ego and pride. For Shīfu, the practice was an integral part of every fiber of his being; physical form was a natural extension of a deep-seated grace within. *His* movements, so fluid and so powerful, were an expression of his cultivation of *qi*, life-force energy, just as water fits the shape of whatever container it is poured into. Though peaceful by nature, he could have used *gōngfu* to subdue any opponent, but in the end, surrounded by Red Guards, he had understood the times for what they were and had made a conscious decision to surrender. I saw the calm in his face before his death.

I wanted to cultivate the same power and grace I had seen in the master but did not know how far I could take the practice on my own. When I had been in Shīfu's presence I had not been ready for his teachings, and now that I wanted to learn, I found myself on the harsh, unforgiving frontier. How would I find a teacher here? We have a saying in Chinese that when a student is ready the teacher will appear. I did not know what being ready meant or how I could be ready, but I decided that night that I would do everything in my power to prepare myself for further guidance.

Unlikely though it was that I would make much progress practicing qigong on my own, the idea of working towards something concrete gave birth to a small hope that dispelled the fears a little. For the first time in a long time, I felt cautiously optimistic, and I fell into a deep sleep.

The next morning, though I had slept very little, I got up before dawn and walked away from the other *gers*. Looking around me in the half-dark, I took in the familiar shape of the distant hills to the east silhouetted against the gentle pink of the approaching dawn. To the west, I saw the dark curves of the river: black-glistening and inscrutable by night, it burbled cheerfully and ran clear by day.

Bending my knees and distributing the weight evenly across the soles of my feet, I noticed that I was breathing shallowly like a fish out of water. I focused on allowing the breath to arise naturally from the *dāntián*. At first, my movements were slow and awkward, but as I progressed through the warm-ups, I found that my body remembered the practice better than my conscious mind. Gradually, I relaxed into the movements and felt my limbs loosen, warmed by the internal heat that arose from the conscious circulation of *qi* in my body. The hem of my *deel* grazed the tips of the new summer grass as I turned, stooped and lunged in sequences my mind recognized only after my body had produced them.

The countryside had changed me. Softness from a lifetime of city living had been replaced by a weathered strength I had never imagined possible though I had glimpsed its potential at the height of my qigong practice as an adolescent. After constant exposure to the wind, cold and sun, my forehead, nose and cheeks had taken on the permanent red glow that colored the herders' faces. After long months of wrangling animals, carrying heavy milking buckets, hauling water, washing, sorting and combing cartfuls of wool and cashmere, the muscles in my back, arms and legs were firm and full of spring. Though no longer an adolescent, my body felt powerful; I lifted loads that weighed as much as I did and handled half-domesticated animals that were many times my size.

As I moved, my tears dropped onto the delicate blades of new grass beneath my feet. Allowing myself to feel Xiǎomèi's pain, her subsequent departure, or Poet's death would have made living in exile impossible. I also could not allow myself to miss the city, my home. Practicing qigong again in the early dawn light, however, I remembered the joy that the practice had brought me as a child. Though Shīfu never officially accepted me as his student, he had seen and quietly supported my passion all along or else he would not have allowed me to join his students or observe him in his teachings and healing sessions year after year.

As I moved deeper into the practice, the peace that I had known while practicing in Shīfu's courtyard came to me again, and I remembered something he had often reminded his students: we conserve energy when we go with the natural flow of the universe; fighting against what we cannot change is nothing but a waste of energy. I did not know what the future would bring, but if I could accept what was right in front of my face no matter what happened to me or to those around me, no matter how much we lost, I could be at peace.

Shīzi and Banhar had come with me when I walked away from the *gers* that morning. Eyes bright, mouths hanging open in wide dog grins, they played together endlessly. Chasing each other in wide arcs around me, tussling on the ground and growling with mock aggression, they were the very embodiment of joy in the growing light of dawn, and I could not keep from smiling, watching them.

From that day on, the dogs and I walked out beyond the *gers* and greeted the sun every morning with my practice and their play.

# Dinner with the Americans
## Beijing, 2005

"Why don't you wear this one tonight?" Malcolm ran his hand down the length of a glimmering silk sheath hanging in Natalie's closet. She glanced up from her book in surprise. Malcolm had spotted the wine-colored *qípáo* she had bought on impulse many months ago from a small boutique shop in Wǔdàokǒu. It had hung unworn in her closet all this time.

"I'm not going out tonight," she said.

"I'm meeting some of your compatriots—people from Missouri. Why don't you come along," he said, draping the dress over her lap. "We're leaving at seven." Natalie had come to know that sleepy-eyed smile very well. The yoga business aside, it was the first time he had invited her to join him for anything work related. She was not particularly interested in meeting American businesspeople, but she was curious about the work that took Malcolm away from Beijing more often than not.

The restaurant in the Cháoyáng district almost hurt the eyes with its flashy crimson and gold décor. It had all the elements of a modern and prosperous China: a sloping tiled roof over the entranceway, the hostess's clingy red *qípáo*, a paw-waving porcelain cat on the front counter. It did not seem like the kind of restaurant Malcolm would normally frequent, but Malcolm was still a bit of a mystery in many ways. One never knew what he might or might not do.

Seeing Malcolm, the young hostess smiled flirtatiously and

with obvious recognition. She led them to a *bāojiān* at the back of the restaurant where they would be able to enjoy their meal in a room of their own away from the other patrons. Though it was still fairly early in the evening, the restaurant was ringing with the boisterous conversations of dozens of diners whose tables were covered with gleaming dishes of braised meats, crispy-skinned duck, butterflied shrimp, whole chickens cut into sections, tofu covered with red chilies, and whole fish whose tails drooped over the edges of the platters they rested on. Tall Yanjing beer bottles and *báijiǔ* glasses accumulated in proportion to the piles of bones dotting plastic red tablecloths. The *bāojiān* with its gentle, ambient lighting was a much-welcomed contrast to the brightly lit main dining room. Gold-tasseled red lanterns hung from tall stands in two of the corners, and silk scroll paintings of cranes and peacocks adorned the walls alongside chrysanthemums, peaches, and cloud-misted mountain landscapes. In the center of the room, a large round table that could comfortably seat eight was covered with a red cloth tablecloth.

Malcolm and Natalie took the hosts' seats facing the door while a waiter in a satin red vest poured tea for them then respectfully backed out the door, closing it gently behind him. Accustomed to the comfort and freedom of yoga clothes, Natalie felt formal and constrained in the tight-fitting silk sheath. Malcolm was looking quite sharp, as always, in a dark gray suit made of fine Italian wool. His arm was draped casually over the back of her chair, and he was looking her over with an appraising smile. She had twisted her unruly mane into a low chignon and had put on some lipstick and eye make-up to go with the dress. Their first meeting aside, he had never seen her with make-up, and apparently he liked what he saw because his smile grew as he ran his fingers lightly up the back of her bare neck. He seemed just about to lean over to kiss her where his fingers had been when the door opened and the hostess led a plane-rumpled, deer-in-headlights couple into the room.

The broad-faced woman was solidly built and endowed with an ample bosom. Dark, unruly curls framed an earnest face. The man was tall, barrel-chested and balding. They looked to be in their late thirties or early forties and had the fleshy pink look of well-fed Midwesterners who spent most of their time indoors. They did not look like typical American businesspeople: the woman could have been a teacher or nurse in her sensible, patterned navy dress, and the man with his polo shirt and slacks looked like he spent most of his time in front of a computer.

When Malcolm introduced Natalie as a "friend" they smiled but looked at her with the vague apprehension that many foreigners gave restaurant waitstaff. Natalie recognized the insecurity of white people who found themselves in China but who did not know how to speak Chinese. She also noticed that instead of seeing her, they looked through her. She was still not sure why Malcolm had brought her along and wished it was just the two of them tonight, but she smiled politely and busied herself with pouring tea for everyone.

To Natalie's surprise, Malcolm spoke to the couple in very good English. *Their* communication had always been in Chinese, but she saw now that Malcolm spoke English fluently and confidently despite a pronounced accent. It was obvious he was comfortable communicating in the language which made his refusal to speak to her in English puzzling.

After Malcolm sent the waitress off with their orders, the man glanced at his wife and cleared his throat. He started to say something in a low voice about having brought something that Malcolm had requested, but Malcolm waved his words away with a jovial smile and an ultra-casual, "Let's eat first. You've come a long way. Relax and enjoy your first meal in China. We'll talk business later." They both sat back and seemed at once relieved and disappointed. The man cleared his throat again in the silence while his wife glanced at the silk paintings on the walls as if looking for something to anchor her.

"What do you do?" she asked, finally turning to Natalie.

"I teach yoga."

"Oh—you have yoga here? I didn't realize China has things like that."

"It's becoming more popular. Are you interested in yoga?"

"Well, I have to admit I don't know much about it. There are classes at the gym, you know, but it's always so hard to find the time to exercise," she said with the apologetic embarrassment of someone who knew she should do more to stay in shape but for whom it was not really a priority. As Natalie's life was dedicated to yoga and other healthy pursuits, she could not think of anything to say to the woman that would not offend or sound presumptuous. She had never been much of a conversationalist, and she had no personal connection with the Midwest, much less Missouri. If it had not been for Malcolm and his business, she never would have met this couple, and she likely would never see them again after this evening. How many thousands of people pass through one's life unacknowledged, and how did one find connection among the brief meetings?

"China has its own systems of exercise, doesn't it?" the man asked. "Tai-chi, chi-gong and such?"

"Yes, but to be honest I don't know much about those practices."

"Oh." He sounded a little disappointed.

"Where did you learn yoga?" the woman asked with a bright smile.

"The Bay Area."

"The Bay Area? Which part of China is that?"

"The *San Francisco Bay Area*," Natalie said. "That's where I'm from." She kept her face neutral and waited for the couple to understand. It was a conversation she often had in China with Americans who assumed she was Chinese-Chinese, and with the occasional Chinese who assumed she was Chinese in the same sense that they were Chinese.

"Oh! You're Chinese American! I was about to say—you speak English beautifully!" the woman exclaimed, evaluating Natalie with new eyes.

"Were you born in China?" the man asked.

"No—born and raised in the States. I came here about a year ago."

Malcolm, silent throughout the exchange, was regarding both sides with amusement as if Americans making small talk was a spectator sport. His fingertips slowly circled the bottom of the teacup he held loosely with both hands. He had ordered Tsingdao beer for his guests.

"I don't know if Malcolm told you, but we're from Rolla, Missouri and there really aren't many Oriental folks where we live," the woman said. "All this has been quite a leap for us. We tried to find out as much as we could about China and Chinese culture before coming here because, you know, we really should know more about your culture. We have three Chinese restaurants in town and Rod suggested that we try all three of them—that was quite an adventure! I even went to the local library to find some books on China but it was all about ancient Chinese history. Thank goodness for inter-library loans!" Suddenly self-conscious, the woman glanced at her husband who took her hand under the table. She looked down then back up at Natalie. "You Chinese women have such *gorgeous* skin. Hon," she said turning to her husband, "Have you ever seen such radiant skin? I wonder if it's genetic. What do you do to keep your skin so beautiful?" She gazed at Natalie with such an odd mixture of admiration and longing that Natalie looked away. Was the woman interested in the names of products, or did she want lifestyle tips, the first of which would be to practice yoga and go vegetarian? Malcolm, as if reading her thoughts, finally chimed in.

"Maybe it's the yoga. And Natalie is a vegetarian. She lives a very healthy lifestyle." He looked at Natalie with the same, small appraising smile as before.

"Oh! I'm sure that's what it is—I'd never thought about that. Maybe we should become vegetarians too. It'd be so hard to give up eating meat though. We do love a good steak, don't we, Hon?"

The woman's husband smiled absentmindedly, his thoughts on something else. He leaned forward, his expression earnest. He could be an accountant—he had a numbers crunching air about him. "So if you were born in the States, were your parents or grandparents originally from China?"

To Natalie's relief, two waiters in glossy red satin shirts entered just then with the chilled appetizers. They perfunctorily rattled off the names of the dishes in Chinese, bowed, and closed the door behind them. "Do you eat jellyfish?" Malcolm asked then chuckled when he saw his guests' faces. "Just kidding! These are clear noodles made from bean starch, and this is shredded tofu in a special sauce. Completely vegetarian. No animals in these dishes." He winked a smile in Natalie's direction. She had never seen him so animated.

The dishes came quickly one after another: three delicacies soup with sizzling rice, sautéed Mongolian beef, barbequed spareribs with pineapple, jumbo shrimp with black pepper, ginger flavored free-range chicken, braised eggplant in a sweet and spicy garlic sauce, and a whole fish that had been deep fried. Malcolm had also ordered stir-fried Chinese broccoli with garlic and Buddha's delight, a mixed vegetables and mushrooms dish, for Natalie. Before long, the Lazy Susan in the middle of the table was completely covered with oil-slicked platters and the room filled with the aroma of cooked meat. Malcolm had ordered well. There was nothing too strange to a Western palate: no braised pig's feet, marinated duck tongue, or scalloped kidneys. There was, however, enough food to feed a large family.

"If there's one thing Chinese people know, it's how to eat," Malcolm proclaimed cheerfully. With typical Chinese hospitality, he urged his guests to try this or that and to eat ever more. He himself ate very little, Natalie noticed, and she wondered if it was because he dined with clients like this on a regular basis.

When they had finished eating, many of the dishes still looked virtually untouched. The couple surveyed the table. "This is so much better than those restaurants we tried back in Rolla. Now this is what Chinese food is supposed to taste like! I don't know if I'd be able to make authentic Chinese food at home though—it looks rather complicated. It would be such a pity to waste all this wonderful food," the woman said.

"Take it back to your hotel," Malcolm said. "You can have it for breakfast."

The man laughed. "There's enough for breakfast, lunch *and* dinner. I guess we could fit some of this in the mini bar." He sat back with a sigh, his hand on his beer glass, but the woman sat forward in her chair. She looked like she wanted to say something but did not know how to broach the topic.

Malcolm casually reached into the fine Italian leather briefcase he always carried with him and pulled out a single photograph. He handed it to the woman with a smile, his eyes fixed on her face.

The woman's breath caught as she took the photo. Her face was filled with such naked longing that Natalie looked away.

It was a Chinese baby, a girl.

"Our baby. Isn't she beautiful?" the woman whispered, tears filling her eyes. The man leaned closer to look, his arm curving protectively around his wife's shoulders.

He nodded and cleared his throat. "Where is our baby now? When can we see her?"

"Tomorrow. You'll see your new baby tomorrow. We'll take care of everything in the morning."


Malcolm's black Audi slid through Beijing's brightly lit streets like a sleek nocturnal animal on the hunt. The city was still very much awake at ten at night, and many of the brightly lit restaurants they passed were filled with late diners. As nighttime Beijing whirled by, Natalie caught snapshots of lives they passed: people caught in mid-speech or in exaggerated laughter. Family celebrations, business meetings, toasts all around. Lives she bore witness to but would never know more about.

"I didn't know you helped American couples adopt Chinese orphans," she finally said.

"You never asked."

"You said you were in the import and export business."

"I am. We import Americans and export babies." She could see the profile of his grin as he kept his eyes on the road.

"That's not funny: babies are not commodities."

"Of course not. But when one gets down to the nitty-gritty details of each transaction—procedures, paperwork, official approval—it basically comes down to the same thing."

Natalie thought about the longing she had seen in the woman's face. How long had they waited, and how much paperwork had they filled out before they could finally come to Beijing to claim their baby? What internal and external obstacles had they needed to overcome before they made their decision to adopt a Chinese baby? Underlying all the paperwork and official red stamps, there was a couple's desire to nurture a little human being no matter how far they needed to travel physically or culturally. It was poignant work, yet Malcolm's attitude bordered on being cavalier.

"It doesn't seem strange to you that you talk about human beings like they're objects you bring to market?"

Malcolm waited several moments before replying. "There are thousands of unwanted children in China. There simply aren't enough Chinese couples who want to adopt. The children need homes and these foreigners have homes and want babies. I bring them together."

"You're doing everyone a favor. I think you must earn a very good living doing this."

He smiled. "The money's not bad."

"Would you be in this line of work—helping people—if you never earned a single cent?"

Malcolm laughed out loud then reached over to chuck her lightly under the chin. It was an annoying gesture that she tolerated for some reason. "Little American, money is everything. This is the new China. I like helping people, but I need to make a living too."

Malcolm fell asleep quickly that night after peeling off Natalie's silk dress and making love to her, but Natalie lay awake long into the night thinking about the couple and their baby. When she finally drifted off, her dreams were filled with babies. Riding through the streets of Beijing, she saw babies everywhere: couples with strollers, young mothers playing with their babies, grandparents watching babies in parks. She arrived at a blockish, official looking building in front of which a Chinese flag flapped briskly in the breeze. Natalie climbed the stairs and entered through metal-framed glass doors. No one greeted her at the front desk, and there was no one was around. At the end of a long hallway, a set of heavy double doors like those delineating hospital wings blocked her view. The doors swung open easily, however, and she entered a cavernous room filled with hundreds of metal cribs lined up in neat rows. Each of the cribs held a baby dressed in a colorful outfit. The spots of color were in sharp contrast to the stark, barren white walls that stretched so high above them that Natalie could not see the ceiling, yet instead of lending the orphanage a feeling of spaciousness, the walls felt oppressive.

Natalie startled when a strident factory bell cut through the silence and a troupe of Chinese nurses wearing little white caps filed in. They moved among the rows feeding some of the babies, changing others. They administered shots, thick needles piercing delicate baby skin, but some babies they tossed unceremoniously into large bamboo baskets following a cursory inspection. The nurses were brisk and efficient, and they ignored Natalie. Within a few minutes, they had made their way through the entire room. Another bell sounded, and the women strode out the door on the other side of the room dragging the large bamboo baskets after them.

They had worked in silence, and the babies had allowed themselves to be handled in silence. Once the nurses were gone, the room was so still that Natalie peered into the crib closest to her then drew back so quickly that she bumped into the crib behind her. All the babies were girls, and they all had flawlessly smooth skin because they were made of white marble. Like the famous terracotta warriors, each one had unique features and a slightly different expression, yet every single one of their mouths gaped open in wails that would never be heard.

*Wú and the young woman are walking past the bǐng and soymilk vendor's cart. The stacks of flaky pastries and the plastic bags of soy milk behind a clear plastic partition are already gone by this time of day, and the seller has gone home to rest. Wú greets neighbors sitting on low stools outside their doorways scrubbing laundry in plastic basins or cleaning large, leafy heads of báicài. They nod at her and look at the young woman with curiosity.*

*"I know my mother's hurts better than I know my own," the young woman tells Wú. "My mother was born in Beijing. She became an orphan after both her parents died when she was very young. Or that is what they told her. I think she was an illegitimate child. Her aunt was reluctant to take her in because she was a girl and they already had four children of their own, but they took her with them when they fled to Taiwan.*

*"My mother always says she was from a very good family in Beijing, but she married beneath her because her aunt just wanted her married off. They saw that my father's family had money so she would be well-provided for. That was enough for them."*

*"Did you come here for your mother or for yourself?" Wú asks the young woman.*

*The younger woman is quiet as she considers the question. "I want to be less of a disappointment to her," she says.*

# Riding Lesson

## Inner Mongolia, 1970

"You need to know how to ride, living here," Bayaraa said to me one day. He had arrived a little earlier in the afternoon than usual, and he was leading a dun-colored mare with a flowing black mane. While I admired horses for their grace and strength, and I admired the ease with which the Mongolians managed their mounts, I had never learned to ride in the almost two years I had lived in the countryside. I worked with animals every day and could handle them as well as any Mongolian by then, but leading them to water or tethering them to be milked was very different from actually sitting astride one and trusting that it would not immediately buck me off. While I respected the animals, there was some comfort in knowing that I was still in charge because of my human cleverness. Riding, however, meant entrusting my life to a horse: one false move could cripple either or both of us for life or worse.

"Thank you," I said to Bayaraa, "I have two good legs that take me everywhere I need to go."

"When you learn to ride you can travel farther and faster. There's a beautiful lake half a day's ride from here that you should see. I can't show it to you unless you learn to ride," he said. "This mare is very tame. Come over to her left side so you don't startle her." I reluctantly walked up to the horse. She was a beautiful animal, her glistening coat freshly groomed. The expression in her eyes was both intelligent and gentle, but I had no intention of riding her. Bayaraa was waiting with his usual patience, however, so I held out a hand.

The mare dipped her velvety nose down to my palm then backed up, shifting uneasily. Bayaraa spoke to her soothingly in Mongolian and slowly stroked her neck. "She can sense your fear," he said. "It's natural that you are both cautious at first, but you will soon learn to trust each other. The relationship we have with our horses is truly special—we cannot live without them. They give us food, drink, strength, and speed. They even give us music."

The mare relaxed as Bayaraa spoke, sensing that she was with a person who understood her. All the Mongolians I knew had grown up around horses and most of them had learned to ride even before they had learned to walk. They had a deep respect for their animals, particularly their horses, but there was a calmness and steadiness about Bayaraa that made him particularly good with the animals. He seemed to understand them on another level and they, sensing this, trusted him. His reputation for soothing even the most skittish and spirited animals was such that he was often called to help with horses that no one else could handle. After regularly spending time with Bayaraa over the past two years, I knew why the animals trusted him. There was a solidity about him as well as a feeling of openness, as if he gave one space to exist. I understood, as the mare understood, that he would never force me to do anything I did not want to do. He seemed so confident that with time and patience I would come to understand the mare and learn to work with her that I felt my own confidence growing.

Bayaraa took my hand and placed it on the mare's neck so I could feel her warmth and strength. The gesture, so simple, threw me into great confusion. Nothing in my life had prepared me for the tangle of emotions and sensations that washed over me. Back in the city, not only had I been too young to consider romance, but all my passion had been channeled into class struggle and the building of a socialist society. Sentimentality had no place in the life of a mission-driven soldier, and my usefulness was measured by how much I could accomplish for the greater good. My male comrades were fellow soldiers, and the feeling between us was that of brothers in arms. In our work together, they never made any special allowances for the fact that I was a woman, nor did I want to be treated differently.

Communism brought equality to women by demanding that we take our places alongside men in the factories and in the fields, but this equality stripped us of our femininity which was regarded as a weakness if not outright liability. We could be strong, independent, assertive and productive, but softness, beauty, and emotional connectivity were considered indulgent and bourgeois, so the women of my generation buried these qualities deeply within ourselves. Moreover, not only were modern women expected to work alongside men, but we were also the mothers of future soldiers and workers. Our bodies and reproductive abilities had been commandeered for the cause.

I had always assumed that I would one day do my part as a woman: I would marry one of my comrades and we would have children who would work for social progress just as I did. While some of my peers had been titillated by the romances that developed between comrades or had "talked about love," *tán liàn'ài*, romantic love never held any allure for me because my passion and allegiance were reserved solely for my country. Furthermore, the fact that the budding relationship between Xiǎomèi and Poet had been curtailed almost as soon as it had begun forever linked romance with tragedy in my mind.

In the countryside, humans and animals carried their virility as naturally as they carried every other natural phenomenon. Birth, reproduction, and death were accepted as a part of the natural flow of life. Unlike the Han Chinese men I had known my whole life, Bayaraa, like the other Mongolians I knew, accepted the human body with its reproductive functions, sexual desires, and myriad emotions without shame. Far from Beijing, the epicenter of ideological discourse, we were free to explore parts of ourselves that had long been suppressed, but it was still not easy for me to shed my reserve enough that I could trust a man with my heart, even a man like Bayaraa who had shown himself to be a true friend and ally. Though I had learned to live like the Mongolians, I was still very much Han Chinese on the inside. Crippled by the modern denial of my femininity on one hand and bound by centuries of restrictive and oppressive female roles on the other, I did not know how to be a woman. I did not know what to do about the unsettling yearnings that crept over me as our friendship developed.

I kept reminding myself that Bayaraa was a Mongolian. That we had become good friends was a testament to his openness as well as to my own adaptability. Even if there had not been significant cultural differences between us, I was constantly mindful of the fact that my stay in the countryside was a temporary one. I did not know whether or when it would be possible, but I held a closely guarded hope in my heart that I would be allowed to return to the city one day. How could I embark on something meant to last a lifetime when I hoped to leave some day?

Flooded with a plethora of emotions and thoughts, I steeled myself and did what I always did: I ignored the discomfiting emotions, buried the troubling thoughts, and focused on action. Establishing a relationship of mutual trust with the mare was more tangible and straightforward than worrying about the murkiness of relationships between men and women.

"Show me how to ride," I said to Bayaraa. He held the stirrup for me as I hoisted myself into the saddle. It was both terrifying and exhilarating to be perched so high up, and the mare's strength beneath me made my heart race. The mare, on her part, bunched her legs beneath her as she prepared to bolt.

"*Za, zats,*" Bayaraa said to her soothingly, keeping a firm hold on the bridle as she jostled sideways. "Loosen the reins—there is no need to pull them so tightly," he said. Then he looked up at me and put a hand on my boot. "Are you alright?" he asked. I looked back at him but could not speak. Never in my life had I felt so immobilized.

After an eternity in which I looked at him and he looked back at me, I slid out of the saddle and mumbled something about continuing the lesson another day. I could not look at him again. I wanted to go hide in the *ger* but my legs refused to move. When he touched my arm, I realized I was shaking and could not control what my body was doing.

*"Yaasen bei,"* he asked softly and brought me in for a gentle embrace, but his kindness only made the shaking worse until I was not only trembling but sobbing. All my life I had been the *tiě gūniáng*, girl of iron, who did not know feminine weakness. I had carried the mantle of imperviousness for so long, yet the harder I tried to be strong and the more I clamped down on the bewildering emotions, the more I shattered into a million pieces.

Bayaraa held me and spoke soothingly in Mongolian just as he had spoken to the mare moments before. Completely unable to control myself now, my body heaved with great sobs, and if he had not been holding me up, I would have collapsed to the ground, curling into myself, a weeping mess. I was deeply ashamed of my lack of self-control and weakness, but I could not stop the sobbing, and I was utterly powerless against the fears that rolled over me: fear of losing control, fear of the potent emotions that washed over me, fear of being seen and known for an aspect of myself that I had never known myself. As I wept, all the grief I had not allowed myself to feel overtook me: I grieved for a mother I never had from whom I could have learned to be a woman, a father I had betrayed, the neighbors I had persecuted, the dear friends I had lost.

Bayaraa did not shrink from the intensity of the storm. He stood quietly, holding me up, allowing me to experience what I needed to experience. When the worst of the storm had passed, shame and embarrassment replaced the fear and grief, but Bayaraa continued to hold me with the gentleness and steadiness I had come to know so well. Some time passed before I was able to straighten myself up and take a step away from him.

"You want a woman, but I don't know how to be a woman," I told him finally.

"What is there to know? I know you, and I admire your spirit. I knew you were a good person the first time I saw you even if you were wrongheaded."

"You are also very stubborn," I observed.

"My family often reminds me of that. I must speak up when things are not right just as I speak up for what is right," he replied. I thought about all the times he and I had butted heads over our work; he had always acted and spoken with complete integrity regardless of whether his views were popular or not.

"I thought I was fighting for what was right, but now I am not sure about anything." It was the closest I had ever come to apologizing for my arrogance. "I have always been so strong," I continued with some effort, "but now I am afraid. You are not afraid of anything."

"I have been afraid many times," he said with one of his rare smiles, "but I have learned to live with fear. It is a friend that brings important lessons.

"I died once. It was the winter of my eighth year. I was alone with the horses, and in my inexperience I did not know that a storm was approaching that would cut me off from where my family had set up camp. One moment it was sunny and clear, but within twenty minutes we were surrounded by a blizzard so thick I could not see two meters in front of my face much less any of the horses. A more experienced herder would have stayed put and waited until the storm blew over, but I was terrified and could not think clearly. I foolishly rode around in the storm looking for our horses, but it was not long before I could not feel my face or any of my limbs.

"When I realized the danger I was in, I gave up control. I prayed to *Tengger* to have mercy on me and let go of the reins. My horse was not only very intelligent, but she was strong. After

I lost consciousness, she found the rest of the horses. She squeezed herself into the middle of the herd, and that is how we both survived the storm. When my family found me, I was still in the saddle but half-frozen. They thought they had lost me.

"I died that day. I went somewhere very light, beautiful, and peaceful, but then I had to come back because it was not my time to go yet.

"Since that time, I have not been afraid of death. It is a part of life. Now, when I feel afraid, I remember that I am still alive in spite of everything. If it is my time to go, I will go. But not until then." Bayaraa looked at me, his face serene. "Not everything you are afraid of will hurt you," he said.

I wanted so much to accept his invitation. "Your horse saved your life," I said looking into the gentle eyes of the mare he had brought me. Now that I was calmer, she was calm as well.

"Our horses have saved our lives too many times to count. It is why we have such a deep love for them." He held the reins out for me to take. "This mare will be a good companion for you for many years to come. When you understand our horses, you will understand us as well."

I took the reins thinking about his words: for many years to come.

# Inner Mongolia



MALCOLM REACHED ACROSS THE bed where they lay on their sides facing each other. Dipping a finger in the condensation on his glass, he traced a wet line from the center of Natalie's forehead down to her chin. She closed her eyes. This was nice. He was gone so often that their time together always felt fleeting, like they were ships passing in the night. Such moments were rare between them, and she wished she could stay here forever with him.

When Natalie opened her eyes, she saw that Malcolm was studying her face, his own expression unreadable. She looked back at him, holding his gaze, searching for something. The intimacy of the moment was undeniable, but she still never felt as if she really knew him. She looked down at her glass. She was both a little relieved and a little disappointed when he broke the silence.

"So, Little American, what do you think of Inner Mongolia so far?"

She had romanticized the Mongolian steppes. Mournful and solitary nomadic song, a silk-robed singer with his horse head fiddle alone on the grassland surrounded only by lush green grass and sheep in the distance. When Malcolm invited her to Inner Mongolia for the long weekend, she had not envisioned Hohhot's urban bustle, chaos and traffic. The shops they passed were filled with touristy trinkets—refrigerator magnets, Mongolian yurt keychains, porcelain camels—and the performance they attended that evening felt artificially "ethnic": stiff smiles on the dancer's faces, gaudy polyester costumes, a nationalistic song about a warhorse galloping to defend the homeland border. Most of the songs had translated names like "Sweet Grassland," "Morning on the Grassland," and "Maiden of the Grassland." Natalie wondered if Mongolians had many names for their home just as the Inuit were reputed to have hundreds of words for snow, but it all came out as "grassland" in translation.

Natalie had hoped to see more than the stereotypical Chinese version of Mongolian culture where the locals, like most minorities in China, were known for their traditional singing and dancing. Modern-day herders and their urban counterparts did not wear brightly colored ethnic costumes as they went about their day-to-day business, but when Natalie glanced around at the Chinese audience she had seen only unquestioning enjoyment of the staged production. It was what they wanted to believe about one of the largest minority groups in the country.

The night she and Malcolm had met at Sandglass Café the music had touched her deeply. Maybe it had been the setting or the small size of the ensemble. Maybe, two years ago and freshly arrived in China, she had been ready to be impressed. Glancing over at Malcolm during the performance, she noticed with relief that he looked unimpressed, bored even. Sensing her look, he had raised his eyebrows at her. It was not what he had anticipated either. On their way to the restaurant afterwards he asked her if she had ever balanced four stacked bowls on her head during yoga practice like the Mongolian contortionist they had seen.

"You're very quiet tonight," Malcolm said. "Didn't you enjoy the last act?" Natalie laughed and threw a pillow at him. At the end of the performance, the air became charged with expectancy as the conductor came on stage and bowed formally to the audience. Two dozen horse head fiddle musicians poised their bows for action, their faces as pale as their white satin shirts: the grand finale promised to be impressive. The conductor raised his arms, and the last act began with slow, pensive, drawn-out notes. Then the stage lights began flickering purple and blue in time to a rigorous beat, and the musicians launched into a lively horse head fiddle rendition of Michael Jackson's "Thriller." The audience erupted into enthusiastic applause that hid Natalie's laughter. The musicians looked as earnest as if they were playing a tribute to their mothers.

"Don't tell me you're a Michael Jackson fan!"

"Why not?" Malcolm sounded genuinely puzzled. "I thought all Americans loved Michael Jackson. The man is so rich he can do anything he wants. People line up to wipe his butt. Go ahead—laugh. He's not the King of Pop for nothing!" Ignoring her laughter, he continued, "He was one of the first Western rock stars I ever heard. When I was growing up, the only music we had from the outside was *dǎkǒu* music—American rejects that were shipped to China to be recycled or destroyed. They were called *dǎkǒu* because the CDs all came with notches cut into them because they had been taken out of circulation, but the cuts were on the outer edges of the discs so they were still playable. People started selling this totally foreign music on the black market and we were blown away. It was very revolutionary. For us anyway."

Born in the late 60s while the Cultural Revolution was still in full swing, Malcolm's childhood must have been a grim one. Natalie had never thought about what life was like for him as a child growing up in a Communist China that, until the late 80s, was largely closed off to the rest of the world.

Malcolm drew himself up to sit against the headboard, his legs stretched out in front of him, water glass pressed against his cheek. It was a warm night, but they were both still fully dressed, the smell of cooking oil from dinner still wafting from their clothes. "Things were simpler back then," he told her, looking off into the distance and frowning slightly. "Most of the time we had enough to eat. We even had meat about once a week. Everything was decided for us so there were not many decisions we needed or could make for ourselves. There simply were not the choices kids have these days. I'm sure it was very different from your happy childhood in America," he said without a trace of sarcasm. When he smiled at her, Natalie thought she detected a hint of self-deprecation, something she never thought she would see in a man like Malcolm.

However different life had been for her materially, "happy" was not an adjective that came to mind when Natalie thought about her childhood in the Bay Area. The constant fighting. The enormous McMansion in the suburbs that never warmed up in the wintertime. How much emptier it felt after her father left.

"My father was a teacher," Malcolm continued. "He was labeled a rightist and counter-revolutionary during the Cultural Revolution." He stared into his glass for a long time. "After he died, my mother worked hard to raise me and my sister. My grandmother helped out when she could, but she had to work too. In those early years when schools were still closed, there were many days when my sister and I were left at home alone. My mother hid books for us to read and we both studied as much as we could with the belief that a good education would open doors for us in the future.

"When schools opened up again, there wasn't enough money for both of us to attend school so my mother sent me. My sister was older and, frankly, smarter, but I was the boy. Back then, I took things for granted. My sister never expressed any anger or jealousy—she wouldn't have dared in front of our mother—but as I learned new things and doors were opened for me, I saw how my sister was left behind. I'm not proud to admit this, but when I was really young I looked down on her because she remained ignorant while I continued on with my schooling. It was only later that I appreciated how much she and my mother sacrificed for me." Malcolm drew a deep breath and let it out with a sigh.

"In China, we don't talk about love the way you do in the West. For us, respecting our parents, fulfilling our obligations and doing our duty well *is* love. My mother loved us by disciplining us and giving us everything she could. We express our love and gratitude through hard work and respect. There's no room for sentimentality."

They sat side by side on the bed for a long time in a comfortable silence. It was the most Malcolm had ever shared about his personal life, the most he had ever shown her. After a while, he turned to her and drew his arm around her waist, drawing her closer so she could rest her head on his shoulder.

"Are you ready to see the famous Mongolian grasslands tomorrow? We've heard them sing about it—tomorrow we'll actually see it," he said, his tone reassuming some of its usual lightness. Natalie turned to look at him, but he immediately put a finger over her lips. "People of my generation don't talk about love the way you do in America," he said, his eyes studying her face.

"I want to ask your opinion about something," Natalie said, keeping her eyes on the trail framed by her horse's ears. Her horse plodded listlessly along, bored with both her rider and the path she traveled day in, day out, carrying tourists on her back. "Master Zhu wants me to go in for special teachings. He is offering me a course of study that he reserves only for his most promising students."

Malcolm's mount was a great deal more independent-minded, and he was having trouble controlling her. She snatched mouthfuls of grass growing alongside the trail and purposely rubbed her flank—and Malcolm's leg—against passing tree trunks. When Malcolm finally managed to get the mare's nose out of another clump of grass, he turned to Natalie. "So? Why do you think he's being so generous with you?" Although she knew he was not exasperated with *her*, Natalie winced at his tone.

"I think he's sincere. He's taught me a lot and has helped me work through many things. He's always been very generous with me," she said, trying to work through the thick morass of her thoughts.

"What's the issue then?" he asked, but he was distracted and not really hearing her.

The day had begun so well. They had known each other for almost two years, and last night was the first time it did not feel as if they were just business partners and occasional lovers whenever he breezed through Beijing. Last night Malcolm had been attentive and open, and there had been a tenderness in their lovemaking. That it had taken them so long to reach this point made the fleeting connection all the more poignant.

The previous night's intimacy had burned off by mid-morning, however. The more Natalie tried to engage Malcolm, the less he responded. The idea of a horseback ride out on the Mongolian steppes had sounded romantic and idyllic when they had planned it in the comfort of their hotel room, but the actual ride out on the open grassland in the middle of a hot summer day was turning into a very long, sunbaked ordeal. It had been pleasantly cool when they started that morning, and Natalie had loved being out on the open, rolling green landscape that was dotted with white sheep specks in the distance, but the novelty of the experience soon wore off as the sun rose quickly in the cloudless sky and they were still riding, hour after hot hour. Natalie wondered how the herdsmen did it, cloaked in their thick robes and exposed to the merciless sun all day long. She kept removing her sunglasses to use the front of her t-shirt to wipe away the sweat that streamed from her forehead. Malcolm was not doing much better although he had picked up a cheap red baseball cap that shielded his eyes from the overly bright landscape. Natalie had teased him about the cap that was so tacky and unlike his usual well-dressed, suave self, but she was not teasing him now.

Natalie thought about Master Zhu's offer. There was something about it that did not feel quite right but she could not put her finger on what it was that bothered her. He had always been very generous with her, but he was also keenly interested in the fact that she was American. He asked almost every time she visited if she could help him make contacts in the States. There was also his relationship to Xiǎo Gāng. Always the solicitous host to her and Dāndān, the magnanimous, self-assured qigong master became a different person whenever his son was present. The last time she and Dāndān visited, he had made Xiǎo Gāng go inside the house while they sat chatting in the courtyard. He had snapped the order at Xiǎo Gāng as if to a troublesome dog. Dāndān had noticed it too—Natalie could tell by the way she had avoided looking at her teacher—but they had not talked about the incident. Maybe every great master needed a thorn in his side to keep him human, but Natalie still could not shrug off the small but irksome misgivings she had about Master Zhu.

Natalie was more than ready to dismount by the time they saw the round, white tops of a small cluster of *gers* in the distance, the white shimmering in the heat. There were corrals for the sheep and a few horses were hobbled together near the *gers*. To the west of the camp, a river wound its way across the grassland like a sparkling ribbon of slow-moving sunlight. According to their travel agent, one of the selling points of the daylong horseback ride was that although it was one of the longest and roughest of the trips they offered, riders could enjoy genuine Mongolian hospitality from the families who lived in the *gers* they passed along the way. Many of these families still depended almost solely on their animals for a living although, the agent had been quick to add, their lives were greatly improved by the education and health care they received in the nearby towns and cities.

"*Nohoi hori!*" the guide called out as they approached, and as if on cue a thickset middle-aged man with a pronounced limp swung open the door to the *ger* closest to them, shooing a black and tan mongrel away from the entrance so they could enter. It felt awkward to just walk into a stranger's home, but the guide had assured her that Mongolians were some of the most hospitable people in the world. As nomads, their lives depended on strangers opening their homes to them and sharing tea, a meal, news, and perhaps a whiff from the traditional snuff bottles some men still stashed in the folds of their *deel*. Clearly, the small, well-maintained *ger* camp had come a long way from its traditional nomadic roots and benefitted from the regular tourist traffic. Even if the hospitality, like the previous night's performance, was completely staged, Natalie was relieved for a chance to be out of the sun for a while. They had been riding for over three hours, and they had only just hit the halfway mark.

Malcolm dismounted awkwardly and walked stiffly into the *ger*. Their Mongolian host frowned slightly when Malcolm sat down on a bed on the right side of the *ger* but Natalie, remembering what she had read in a guidebook, circled the *ger* clockwise to the left and found a seat on the bed next to the oldest woman she had ever seen. The woman's eyes were pearly gray with cataracts, and in her ancient, gnarled hands she held a small whittling knife and a piece of wood that just fit in the palm of her hand. Gazing straight ahead of her, she turned the small piece of wood this way and that, feeling with her fingertips. Small curls of wood dropped onto a handkerchief in her lap as she slowly worked the knife. The old woman wore a plain, blue, cotton Mongolian *deel* and a headscarf of a lighter shade of blue. Her only jewelry was a large silver ring inset with a black-veined, oval turquoise that perfectly matched the color of the sky outside. While Malcolm and the guide discussed the logistics of their trip, Natalie sat quietly next to the old woman and watched her carve. There was no need to speak or make an effort to connect, much as one does not need to befriend a very old tree. She wondered what the old woman had seen and experienced in her lifetime.

Malcolm mopped his brow with a handkerchief and looked around the cramped space for something to say or do. The man was completely out of his element and clearly not comfortable with the fact. He asked questions about the *ger's* construction, wanted to know how many head of sheep and goats they raised, where they went for water, how often they moved in the summertime, trying to get a male fix on their host's situation. The Mongolian man responded to Malcolm's many questions with monosyllabic answers, keeping his attention focused on the food he was preparing. The only time he looked at Natalie—briefly, gravely, directly into her eyes—was when he offered her a cup of milk-tea, his left hand supporting his right elbow in a gesture of respect. Malcolm's alpha wolf posturing, for that is what it was, was not only out of place but silly when contrasted with the Mongolian man's quiet, weathered dignity. Natalie did not know whether to feel embarrassed or sorry for Malcolm.

When the Mongolian man served them *buuz* on a low table in the middle of the *ger*, the smell of the steamed dumplings made her realize how hungry she was. Vegetarian though she was, Natalie did not want to be ungrateful so she ate the flour wrappers of a couple of the dumplings and transferred the meat centers to Malcolm's bowl as discreetly as she could.

The old woman, still carving, did not join them in the meal but spoke briefly to the man in Mongolian. He glanced in Natalie's direction, got up, retrieved a clean blue and white ceramic bowl from the cupboard, and ladled something white and thick from a metal canister next to the door. He handed the bowl to Natalie in the same way he had respectfully handed her the tea, indicating the sugar bowl on the table with his chin. It was the most delicious yogurt Natalie had ever tasted. She ate slowly so she could savor every spoonful.

It was not just the yogurt. It was the coziness of the *ger*, the laconic but not unfriendly Mongolian man, and above all it was the steadfast presence of the old woman who even without sharp eyesight had noticed that Natalie ate very little. All the little irksome things in her life melted away in that peaceful, sheltered space: embarrassment on Malcolm's behalf, disappointment at how quickly the intimacy between them had evaporated, uncertainty about Master Zhu and his role in her life, worries about getting enough clients back in Beijing. None of it mattered in that moment.

After the meal, Natalie walked down to the wide, shallow river that ran to the west of the *ger* camp. The water was so clear that Natalie could see the smooth stones that lined the river's bed. She took off her sandals and walked back and forth in the cold, sparkling water. She felt like a kid again as the knee-high water swirled around her legs. She had come to Inner Mongolia with a vague longing that had been weighing on her for a long time. If questioned, she would not have been able to say what it was she was looking for or what she missed in her life, but it was there at every turn: a dissatisfaction, a discontentment, always an expectation of something more. The previous night with Malcolm was nice. Fleeting moments. But here, standing in the middle of a clear-running river with the sunlight reflecting off the water's surface and into her eyes, she had it: contentment. For a few brief moments, she was happy.

When it was time for them to move on, Natalie went in to see the old woman again. The old woman's face crinkled into a toothless smile as she sensed the younger woman's approach. Reaching out, she pressed the finished carving firmly into Natalie's hand. "For you. A little thing," she said in heavily accented Mandarin.

The carving, though roughly done, was unmistakably not just a horse but a *dancing* horse. Holding the small piece of wood in her hand, Natalie could feel the joy and energy of the dance. She wanted to express her gratitude but no words came. Knowing she would never see the old woman again, she was suddenly filled with a deep sadness.

As Natalie stood wordlessly in front of the old woman, fingering the small carving, the old woman reached for her hands and pulled her towards herself. The ancient hands with their gnarled fingers, thick blue veins and very soft skin were surprisingly strong. Framing Natalie's face in those beautiful hands, the old woman gently sniff-kissed Natalie on the forehead as the younger woman's tears fell into her lap.

*They hear yelling as they approach the bus stop. Everyone is staring at a young couple as they scream at each other, their grievances laid out for the world to hear. She is accusing him of cheating with another woman, and he is saying she is crazy. Wú sighs and shakes her head. She silently says a small blessing for the young people and hopes they will find peace. "It's hard for the young people in this generation to get along with others," she remarks. "With no siblings to share things with, they are all little emperors and empresses. They are used to getting their way and do not know how to make room for others."*

*The young woman looks troubled. "Why are relationships so complicated?" she asks.*

*Wú smiles. "It doesn't have to be complicated. It's natural to hope that someone else's yin will complement our yang or vice versa, but the troubles come when we hope the other person will complete us. That is too much to ask of someone else. We look outside ourselves for what we already have within. We all have yin and yang. It is just a matter of balancing them inside ourselves first."*

*"It is so lonely to live by yourself," the young woman says, musingly.*

*"The sun, the trees, the birds are all my friends. I have lived alone for many years, but I never feel lonely," Wú replies.*

# The Illness



THE FIRE WAS BURNING so fiercely that wispy flame tips reached through the top of the stove like the long, thin fingers of spirits. Herbs boiled briskly in a large wok, filling the *ger* with the bitter smell of medicine that mingled with the incense burning on the table. Bayaraa's face was flushed from the heat, and the sweat on his forehead reflected the stove's winking firelight and the wriggling flame of a single candle. Feeling more dead than alive, I lay on the bed while a great fever raged through me. Every bone in my body ached, and I almost passed out from pain every time I moved.

Afraid that what I had was contagious, the other girl had fled the *ger* on the first day of the fever so Bayaraa had come to stay with me. He bolstered me up with pillows, spoon-fed me broth and medicine, and sponged my face with moist, cool towels. He had removed his heavy winter *deel*, and the thin cotton shirt he wore was soaked with sweat as he nursed me with a tenderness I had come to know well over the past few months. He was not demonstrative or overbearing in any way, but it was difficult for me to accept his help as I was accustomed to being stoic and self-sufficient. I was so sick, however, that I had no choice but to allow him to take care of me.

Bayaraa brought an old woman, a distant relative, to see me. She took a big risk in coming since all superstitious practices were forbidden and she could have been sentenced to death for practicing witchcraft. Everyone stayed away from where there was illness, however, and officials were unlikely to venture out into the deep

150

Mongolian cold to investigate.

Churning on a sea of fever and pain, I caught blurry glimpses of the old woman's strange dress through half-closed eyes. She wore a closely fitted brocade cap on which two almond shaped eyes were embroidered, but her own eyes were completely obscured by thick, black, silk tassels that dangled in a fringe in front of her face. Draped around her shoulders was a blue cape decorated with several rows of multi-colored cloth strips, and a round metal disk covered her chest. She held a wooden staff in her left hand while she rang a bell with her right hand to punctuate the chanting. The only jewelry she wore was a thick silver ring inset with a large turquoise the color of the summer sky. It glinted in the firelight when she moved.

The old woman chanted a mantra over and over in a strange language until the *ger* pulsated with the syllables and the words were burned into my feverish consciousness: *Tayatha Om Bekandze Bekandze Maha Bekandze Randza Samudgate Soha.*

That is all I remember of her visit because it was not long before I succumbed completely to the red heat that engulfed me.

I spiraled endlessly inside a kaleidoscope of a thousand hells. I was plunged into different times and places and experienced things that were not of my own body or consciousness: massive wars fought with technology I had never heard of; entire cities exploding and burning; soldiers massacring thousands of people; animals mutilated and tortured. I had never known that such destruction was possible or that such suffering existed. The depth of the pain possible in this world leveled me completely.

I was a female teacher we had struggled against. I felt her humiliation after we shaved off all the hair from one side of her head then paraded her with the yin-yang head in front of her neighbors and colleagues.

Pain shrieked from the most private and tender recesses of my body when men forced themselves on me in the cold darkness, their breaths reeking of alcohol. My arms and legs pinned to the snowy ground by the men's overwhelming weight, the sense of utter powerlessness was far worse than the pain. Worse still was the shame of being violated in a place so far from my family whom I was afraid to face again. I understood what it meant to have a death wish yet to live on in a young, vital body that was not ready to die.

I knew the darkness that possessed the rapists: I was one of them. Deep resentment towards the Han Chinese who had stripped us of our way of life burned away all that had been tender inside of me. Mad with rage, I was capable of a violence that frightened even myself as I tore the girl's clothes from her body.

I was Poet just as the icy waters of the half-frozen river closed over my face. I saw Xiǎomèi's smile, the delicate lines of the backs of her hands and fingers as they hung the New Year's decorations. My last thought was that it did not matter how many texts I knew. Even death could not erase a coward's shame.

I was my father. My body broken by hard labor and lungs devastated by pneumonia, I wasted away on a hard army cot feeling deep remorse that I had failed to protect my daughter. After my wife died, I had hidden behind my books and lost myself in the alluring idealism of the Western Romantics.

I experienced things of the future.

Men beating women, pulling their hair, choking them.

Crowds numbering in the tens of thousands, surrounded by broken glass and burning cars, fired upon by men wearing uniforms.

Missiles shrieking from the sky, reducing sky blue and gold domed temples into piles of gray rubble.

Tall buildings collapsing into themselves as if they were made of sand, sending up huge plumes of black smoke.

Wounded children who had no living family members, mere skin and bone skeletons in an entire region that had been leveled by bombs. Only a few kilometers away, divided by barriers topped with barbed wire and patrolled by tanks and heavily armed soldiers, the wealthy strolled on the beach and threw away food.

Dark-skinned people locked in cramped, airless, windowless cells.

Light-skinned people contracting in fear when they saw dark-skinned people.

Child soldiers carrying guns as large as themselves.

I experienced life in the spirit realm.

Dull-eyed people went through the motions of living while I, an incubus, rode in their chests. Having entwined myself around a woman's heart, I made her reach into her daughter's chest to mangle *her* heart to leave a mark she would carry for the rest of her life.

I was the red-eyed demon living inside a man who stole more of his children's spirits every time he raped them. I had been inside his father too. The men in his family had been violating their children for decades. Generation after generation, like mirrors that face each other, their pain reflected into an infinity of darkness.

Disoriented by the banging of metal against metal in the water, stabbed repeatedly by sharp spears, I writhed as a large hook imbedded deeply into my back dragged me over the side of a boat where men waited with knives. The water in the cove was red with the blood of my clan that had numbered in the hundreds. We would never again spiral out of the water in joy or play amidst the waves.

I raced for the tree line as a droning plane circled overhead. Though the sky was clear, I heard the crack of thunder, and I could no longer run, my blood staining the snow a bright red. As I drew my last breaths, humans came for my pelt with their knives unsheathed.

My sides heaving, I was not yet dead when men began to carve the heavy tusks from my face.

In river water steeped a deep, chemical red by the discharge from a nearby factory, my gills pulsated as my sides convulsed in final spasms. The crimson water bobbed silver with thousands of carcasses like mine.

Stretching as far as the eye could see, only brown stumps and bleached branches remained of the luxuriant forests that had covered entire mountain ranges. My body, the exposed earth, was the color of dried blood.

The kaleidoscope whirled on, spiraling me deeper and deeper into the heart of all that is. My heart was torn to shreds. I could not shut out the cries of the billions upon billions who were suffering. I saw how much we can lose in this world, how there is no escaping the pain.

After an eternity of being surrounded by shrieking spirits, after spinning inside a million human hells, I eventually realized I was not alone. There was someone with me: a quiet presence who remained by my side even while I was whipped about and wrung out again and again. I heard the rustle of feathers and caught sight of a curved beak and sharp talons. Even from within the insanity of the kaleidoscope, I found that if I concentrated on the silent figure beside me, the chaos became less immediate though I was still plunged into scene after horrific scene.

Then a strange thing happened. We began to move away from the pain. We drifted farther and farther upwards in great spirals as if soaring above the earth on great wings. The shrieking behind us now, my ears rang with silence. I began to see more. I saw lush tropical forests and sparkling alpine rivers. I saw sleek fur and the clear eyes of healthy animals, more luminous and more precious than all the jewels in the world. I wept at the graceful dance of schools of fish as they flashed as one body through the ocean. Birds in V-shaped migration burst my hurting heart open.

I saw spirits playing in forests, streams and grasslands. They dove among ocean waves and rode lightly on the wingtips of birds. Each blade of grass was home to a different spirit.

I was the forest, home to millions of plants and animals, growing back when humans gave me space again.

I was salmon returning to our ancestral spawning grounds after humans removed the dams that had blocked our passage for over a hundred years.

I was wolf returning in numbers to restore balance in our ancestral homes.

I was playful sea otter returning to our ancestral waters to dive for sea urchins. As we return, the kelp forests that sustain life thrive once again.

I was the laughter of a family that had come together to share a meal.

I was the light surrounding an older couple as they relaxed in a long embrace.

I became a child's face opening like a flower when his father spoke kindly to him.

I was the joy and wonder of new parents as they held their new baby.

Higher and higher we flew, spiraling upward on columns of warm air. When I looked down again, I finally understood. Everything I had experienced was a part of a vast, incredibly intricate and constantly changing mandala. Dark and light, lovely and hateful, the world pulsated with change: reds and oranges were replaced by greens and blues in the blink of an eye. In the next moment, the whole thing shimmered in brilliant yellows and a million shades of gold. Graceful, fractal curves and spirals gave way to the orderly, angular lines of crystals. Beautiful symmetry and order broke open for the chaotic profusion of creation.

I could not distinguish where I had been in the pattern, but all that mattered was that I had a place in that pulsating sphere of beauty.

As the eagle and I hovered over the world, I finally felt *their* presence, in the thousands, and I sobbed in gratitude. Every strand of my being recognized my ancestors. I felt their deep love, wisdom, and unconditional support. Bathed in their light, I knew unequivocally that they are always here to help and guide me. I am never alone.

I stayed in that space with the eagle and my ancestors for what seemed like eons as I absorbed the complexity of the magnificent mandala that bound us all together.

Bayaraa told me later that after the fever broke, I became so still he thought I had died. There was no breath in my body that he could detect, and my limbs had grown cold. He wanted to take me to the ancestral charnel grounds for a sky burial. Illegal or not, he told me, his voice cracking, he had wanted the great birds of prey to return my body to *Tengger*.

The old woman stopped him with an upheld hand. She removed the headdress and cape and set down her staff and bell. Sitting cross-legged next to my bed, she closed her eyes in meditation and remained by my side for the next few days. While Bayaraa dozed or rose to keep the fire going, she neither slept or ate and came out of the deep meditation only to drink a little tea.

When I awoke, my eyes opened, just like that, and the first thing I saw was the old woman's face. I had never seen a more beautiful face. Even with the many wrinkles and the disheveled gray hair, she looked neither young nor old. Only infinitely peaceful.

# Medical Procedure

Beijing, 2007

Traffic was backed up by one of the worst accidents Natalie had seen in Beijing. The tangled mess of twisted metal, plastic and broken glass was on Dāndān's side of the taxi when they finally eased by, and though Natalie did not want to look as they passed, she saw enough. A Hongqi sedan was sandwiched between the black Audi that had rear-ended it and the back of a bus. The Audi had slammed into the sedan with such force that the car had spun almost ninety degrees and was crumpled to nearly half of its original width. On the driver's side of the windshield there was a shattered bulls-eye target, a complex spider web etched into glass. Nearby, a three-wheeled cart lay on its side, and the bitter melons it had been carrying were strewn over the road. Blue-uniformed public security officers held gawking onlookers back as medics eased a limp human form from the crumpled Hongqi. Like the drivers ahead of them, their taxi driver slowed down almost to a stop as he gaped at the tangled mess, muttering incredulous expletives under his breath. Natalie hated how people were fascinated by violence and tragedy, like flies attracted to rotting meat.

Dāndān, gazing listlessly out the window, did not react to the scene in any visible way. Two lines were etched deeply between her eyebrows in what had become, in the past few days, a permanent expression. Her long, beautiful dancer's hair was pulled into an indifferent and messy ponytail. She wore no make-up, and dark crescents shadowed the undersides of her eyes.

*"Does Master Zhu know?"*

*"He said it wasn't possible. He told me to take care of it."*

*"But...but how do you feel about that?"*

*"I don't have a choice. If he is opposed, then there's nothing I can do."*

*"It's not what you want. Is it?"*

*Dāndān had not answered. Arms wrapped tightly around her belly, her eyes had sought out Natalie's only briefly before she asked in a small voice, "Will you come with me? I will need help getting home."*

The public hospital had the busy, scattered feeling of a crowded train station. Young and old shuffled up to the registration window while family members waited listlessly on battered plastic orange chairs that were bolted to the floor in immovable rows. When Natalie and Dāndān reached the window, the receptionist was brisk, efficient and indifferent as she recorded Dāndān's information and assigned her a number. Faced with a long and growing line of patients, she frowned when Natalie did not immediately understand what she said. She stood up behind the glass partition and pointed emphatically toward the cashier's window on the other side of the room.

"Pay," she said, curt and impatient. "Then go to the OB-GYN unit. Second floor. Follow the signs." Not waiting to see if Natalie understood, she was already summoning the next person in line. Natalie hated hospitals, and this was her first time inside a Chinese hospital. She squinted at the signage trying to make out the unfamiliar Chinese medical terms. Dāndān was too lost to help navigate. Like a tired, mute, but obedient child, she followed Natalie's lead from unit to unit, floor to floor, up and down the stairs. The ultrasound was performed by a different unit from the one that performed the blood tests, and the OB-GYN doctors were housed on a different floor from either the ultrasound unit or the blood work laboratory. For each new procedure, they needed to go back down to the ground floor to pay the cashier first. Like airports and long-distance bus stations late at night where time becomes an abstraction, the hospital, with its de-humanizing fluorescent lights, pea green walls, and acrid smell of antiseptic and bleach, existed in another, colder dimension where all that mattered was survival. Natalie felt a migraine coming on, but she had only to look at Dāndān holding the pink cashier receipts limply in her hands and staring at nothing in particular to know that if they were to make it through the ordeal it would be through sheer willpower and teeth-gritting endurance on her part.

Many months ago when Dāndān told Natalie about the deep depression she had fallen into after the car accident that ended her career as a dancer, Natalie had found it hard to believe that her friend was ever anything other than happy energy and light. Seeing the blankness in her eyes now, as if the real, beautiful, vivacious Dāndān had merely stepped out, Natalie understood the depths of her despair and realized that the darkness had never gone away on some level. Dāndān had credited Master Zhu with having brought her out of the void at that very low time in her life, but now he had left her in an even deeper abyss.

As the long hospital minutes dragged into hours, the darkness that had overtaken Dāndān seeped into Natalie as well. Natalie felt more and more sluggish as she groped her way through the thick, black fog of the migraine. Struggling to stay focused, she reached into her pocket and found the old woman's horse. As her fingers caressed the rough, unsanded lines, she unclenched her jaw with an effort and tried to breathe slowly so that she could stay present and remain useful. The open, sunlit, lush-green grassland, the peace she had felt inside the *ger*, the old woman's wordless love—it was all very, very far away now.

"He told me to practice qigong to prevent a pregnancy. I did everything exactly as he said so it was a long time before I even began to suspect that I could be pregnant." Dāndān's low voice jerked

Natalie back to the present. They had finally finished the last of the tests and were waiting outside the OB-GYN clinic for the results. It had taken them two and a half hours to get to this point. Still rubbing the little horse in her pocket, Natalie could think of nothing to say.

She had never suspected the two might be lovers, but now she wondered how she could have been so naïve. All the signs had been there: Dāndān's special status among Master Zhu's students, the teachings he reserved only for her, her blind adoration for the man. Dāndān would have done anything for him. If he had promised immortality or supernatural powers, she would have believed him. It must have been very flattering to him—to any man—to have such a beautiful woman so in love with him. The power one human can have over another.

It was a sordid and age-old scenario: how many teacher-student pairings had there been over the centuries? How many teachers had taken advantage of their students' vulnerability and trust? Not long ago, a huge scandal had broken out in the yoga community back home: a well-known yoga icon was accused of sexual harassment by several of his former students. It came to light that he had had several affairs with his students and was divorcing his wife of twenty odd years to marry a former student. *We are all consenting adults*, he had said, denying that he had done anything wrong.

"He's dropped me as his student. I've made him lose face," Dāndān said, once again jolting Natalie out of her thoughts. "Master Zhu is one of the best teachers in Beijing. He's the director of the National Qigong Institute. Without his support, no one else will take me."

Natalie could not hold back any longer. "You're carrying his *baby*. The man has abandoned you. Why would you want the support of someone so utterly selfish?" The women around them stared, and Natalie realized she had spoken too loudly. She immediately regretted the cruelty of launching into Dāndān right when she was most vulnerable and glared at the wall in front of them, her head throbbing with the black heat that threatened to engulf her. Dāndān did not seem much affected by Natalie's outburst, however. She hardly seemed to have heard.

"Maybe he's right. Maybe if I had been more developed or had had better control over my body this would not have happened."

Before Natalie could reply, a nurse emerged from the door of the clinic and called Dāndān's number. The enormity of what Dāndān was about to do suddenly hit Natalie. "Are you sure this is what you want? There are other options. There are so many childless couples out there. Malcolm can help...." But Natalie knew it was useless even as she spoke. Dāndān looked at her with dull eyes and shook her head. She left her things with Natalie and followed the nurse through the door.

It was a relatively simple process, a nurse had informed them earlier in a perfunctory, neutral voice. Thousands of women in China had abortions every day—it was one of the more straightforward outpatient procedures they did. Their hospital alone performed up to a hundred procedures every day from sunup to sundown. Quick, safe and relatively painless, it would last only a few minutes once the local anesthetic kicked in. Natalie imagined Dāndān lying in a windowless room, her feet in stirrups. Such a humiliating, powerless position.

The alternatives would have exacted too high of a price. Master Zhu, though long separated from his wife, was still married. Even if he were allowed to have a second child given Xiǎo Gāng's disabilities, he would not claim paternity for a child born outside of his marriage. Without a legal father and because Dāndān was not originally from Beijing, the child could not be registered under the *hùkǒu* registration system. If Dāndān had the baby and stayed on in Beijing, her child would not be officially recognized as a member of society which in turn would affect their housing, the child's education, health care, and future employment opportunities. Both mother and child would be compelled to always exist somewhere in the margins of society unless Dāndān could bribe an official to get her child the coveted Beijing *hùkǒu*. Yet even if she managed to get the *hùkǒu* for her child, nothing could alleviate the social and familial censure Dāndān would face as a single mother, not to mention the economic hardships she would experience as a young woman who had not finished her university education and who did not have a job. It was not that single motherhood was impossible, but there were many reasons that few women chose to be single mothers in China.

Abortion was an acceptable and expedient option in the case of inconvenient and officially unsanctioned pregnancies. Chinese society was not troubled by any of the moral implications of abortion that preoccupied Western societies. Besides, it was an inexpensive and final solution to Dāndān's predicament. The whole procedure cost about 400 yuan with an additional 300 yuan for the post-abortion anti-inflammatory medications. Even with the medicine, it came to less than ninety US dollars which, though not cheap, was affordable for most urban women.

Natalie wondered if Master Zhu experienced *any* feelings of compunction at all. She remembered the kindness and warmth he had shown her on multiple occasions and could not believe that he was a completely heartless man. On the other hand, she was a trophy student from America who could, he undoubtedly hoped, provide connections to an American market. His treatment of her could not be taken as an accurate indication of his qigong practice or level of spiritual development. Moreover, now that Natalie thought about it, virtually all his private students were young, attractive and female. It was quite possible that Dāndān was not the first to find herself in this predicament.

Dāndān lay curled on her side, her arms wrapped tightly around her abdomen. Most of the beds in the recovery ward were filled, and from time to time the other patients' low groans filled the room. The windows were closed, and the air outside looked heavy and stagnant, the late afternoon sky a hazy smog-orange. The doctors had used a local anesthetic for the procedure, but Dāndān's face was screwed up in pain as the drugs wore off. A few hours ago, she had been anxious but calmly determined. Now, tears poured down her face sideways in streams.

Natalie tried to staunch the flow with tissues but the tears kept coming. She did not know which was worse: the steely silence before the abortion or the raw pain she heard now in the suppressed sobs. Feeling wholly inadequate in the face of such intimate loss—she was not even a sister or family member—Natalie closed her eyes against the migraine and waited.

"The woman was also pregnant," Dāndān finally said.

"Which woman?" There had been many pregnant women in the OB-GYN unit.

"The accident. The woman they pulled out of the car. She was pregnant."

Natalie swallowed. She had seen that the driver of the Hongqi was a woman but had not seen the woman's face or the front side of her body. She wondered if the woman had survived. If *her* baby had survived.

"I wanted the child, Natalie. My whole body wanted the baby. It was instinct and love like nothing I've ever felt before. Even what I feel for Master Zhu is nothing compared to what I felt for the baby."


That night Natalie dreamt that she was a little girl who had stumbled upon *Táo Huā Yuán*, the mythical Chinese Peach Blossom Shangri-La. Row after row of ancient, gnarled peach trees had exploded into bloom as far as the eye could see. The ground was strewn with flower petals that made a soft carpet under her bare feet, and more petals drifted down from the trees all the time, glowing a gentle pink as they floated through rays of sunlight. Filled with the exuberance of the very young, Natalie skipped among the trees catching petals on her tongue. They melted like snowflakes in her mouth, tasting faintly sweet. Her nose filled with the delicate, peach-like fragrance of the blossoms, hints of the fruits to come.

After a time, she arrived at the center of the garden where the largest tree of all rose up grandly, its gnarled branches stretching high above all the other trees. It looked to be as old as China itself. The tree's branches were heavy with fruit at the peak of ripeness, but even the lowest branches were just out of reach. When Natalie arrived at the base of the ancient tree, she saw that hundreds of peaches littered the ground around her. Suddenly ravenous, she stooped to pick one up but realized that none of them had survived the fall. Wide gashes split the downy skin open to expose bruised flesh. What had been the color of sunshine had turned a wretched brown. Natalie's nostrils were filled with the sharp, vinegary smell of rotting fruit.

*At the indoor market, Wú visits the vendors who have the freshest produce and the most reasonable prices. They greet her warmly as they have known each other for years. Xiǎomèi is in her usual place three stalls from the end of the row. Today she is crocheting a tiny cap for her daughter's new baby, a boy, using red yarn. Her hands continue to move even as she smiles at Wú.*

*"You've come," she says cheerfully. "The spinach is not as good today but the gàilán is very fresh. Here—I saved these for you."*

*"You already finished the socks? You work very quickly," Wú says.*

*She smiles as she hands Wú a large bunch of gàilán. "His feet are so tiny it didn't take me more than a few hours," she says. She pushes away the money Wú pulls from her cloth purse. "What! We are old friends. Don't insult me!"*

*"Friendship is one thing, but how are you going to make a living if you keep giving things away? You're a terrible businesswoman!" This is an old and ongoing argument. Xiǎomèi finally accepts the money but hands back the larger bill.*

*"Don't cross me," she says firmly.*

*The young woman had wandered away but joins Wú now in front of Xiǎomèi's stall. "These are for you," she says, indicating a bag heavy with beautiful Yángshān "honey" peaches, full of juice and as sweet as candy.*

*"What?" Wú exclaims. "You don't need to give me anything!"*

*"It's a small token of my appreciation," she says.*

*Xiǎomèi watches the two with interest. "Who is this young lady?" she asks.*

*Wú smiles. "A new friend," she says.*

# The Sun



I WAS JUST WELL enough to sit up when Bayaraa wrapped me warmly in a sheepskin *deel* and lifted me carefully onto his horse before he vaulted into the saddle behind me. Though my body was left completely unmarked by the illness on the outside, I was as weak as a newborn infant, and I had lost a considerable amount of weight. Jostling with the horse's even gait, I fell into a half-conscious state and would have slipped right out of the saddle if Bayaraa had not held me firmly by the satin *bus* that was wrapped tightly around the waist of my *deel*.

We traveled by starlight as there was no moon. By the time we arrived at the base of a small mountain, I could not feel my feet in their fur-lined boots, nor could I feel my hands even though they had been tucked into my sleeves the whole time. The sky to the east glowed gently with the first blush of dawn.

Near the top of the mountain, the old woman had built a fire that was almost as tall as she was and had hot tea ready for us. I accepted a bowl with gratitude and waited for the warmth to reach my toes. No one spoke. Bayaraa and the old woman understood each other without the need for words and I, too feeble to question or to compose a coherent thought, gazed mutely at the dancing flames. Despite the crackling of the fire and the whistling of the wind all around us, a stillness pervaded everything as if Earth herself was holding her breath, waiting.

The old woman stared intently into the high-reaching flames

for a long time, reading them. Then, with a small sigh, she dragged a large canvas bag towards herself and pulled out the brocade cap with the thick, black tassels in the front, the blue cape with its many rows of colorful cloth strips, and the round metal disk she had worn when she performed the healing ceremony during my illness. The bag also contained her wooden staff and the bell she had used to punctuate her chanting. The bell tinkled softly when she laid it on the ground next to the cap, the disk, and the robe. Then, without words or ceremony, she threw everything into the fire one by one just as the first rays of sunlight shot across the horizon.

Holding onto my shoulders, the old woman turned me away from the burning objects so that I faced the rising sun. "You're sad, my child," she said. "It is very normal. Look into the sun's face every morning and see what he has to teach you." Sunlight filled my eyes, and my nostrils were full of the pungent smoke of burning cloth. I nodded, unable to speak. "Follow the waxing and waning of the moon and see what she has to teach you," she continued.

Though I had only just begun to warm up, the old woman motioned for Bayaraa to put me back on the horse and waved us off. With the stallion's nose pointed east the whole way home, we rode with the sun in our eyes.

I did not question anything. Not the long ride to the mountain and back, not the burning of the old woman's healing implements, not the strange instructions. I just felt very tired.

The answers were long in coming. For several months after my recovery, all of life appeared to go on as usual. The other students and I worked with the animals, prepared our meals, mended clothing and tools, even laughed together on occasion. I acted and felt almost the same as before, but there was a difference within myself I could not name. I had come so close to death yet had not died. I had seen things, yet even the most horrible things were, in my memory, as elusive as wisps of smoke. Gone was the intensity and anguish of my illness, but in their place there was a deep, pervasive melancholy I could not shake even when I smiled outwardly. I wanted to see the old woman but Bayaraa would only say, a little cryptically, that she could be found only when she wanted to be found.

A long time ago, Shīfu had told his students about a special qigong practice that only the highly skilled could attempt: sun gazing. *People don't hurt their eyes looking directly at the sun?* his students had asked him, incredulous. *Not if they know what they are doing and they go about it carefully*, he had replied. I had not been overly curious at the time thinking that it was yet another esoteric qigong practice I would never know much less experience. Yet the fact that I had heard about sun gazing from Shīfu so long ago was perhaps the reason I did not question the old woman's instructions. I certainly held no illusions about being a skilled practitioner, but I also did not hesitate to do something that would have seemed, to anyone in their right mind, both strange and very possibly dangerous. I cannot say that I was in my right mind though. Everything I had known and taken for granted was gone. Like a child learning to take its first steps, I was learning how to walk again.

I started sun gazing. As tired as I was after the illness, I managed to get up before the sun rose each morning. Not knowing what to do or what to expect, I sat at the top of a nearby hillock and looked into the sun for a few minutes every morning as it rose. It did not feel harmful, and the ritual of getting up and waiting for the sun every morning was comforting. Dry, windy spring is a hard enough time on the Mongolian steppes, but that spring was an especially difficult one for me. I did not want to talk to anyone, not even to Bayaraa when he came to visit, and the others were wise enough to leave me be. It was clear that the illness had changed me.

Even the most challenging times pass, however. We rebuilt our country after foreign invasions and civil wars. We experienced famines and earthquakes and the horrors of the Cultural Revolution. We were banished into exile together. We lost Xiǎomèi and Poet. I almost died. Things were always shifting, always changing, so it had to happen that with enough time the sadness that had come over me dissipated as well. As the days lengthened and I had to rise earlier to be in place when the sun rose, I felt more and more drawn to the practice and felt compelled to sit for longer periods of time. After several weeks, I was gazing at the sun for an hour, sometimes two hours, every day.

At the beginning, my eyes watered and I had terrible headaches that lasted most of the day. On other days, I broke down and wept for no good reason at all or, bewildering even myself, I became fiercely angry at the smallest things and snapped at people if they were too slow or not careful enough in their work. Many days, I just slept. I finished my work in a half-daze and then crawled back to bed, getting up only for the evening chores when the animals came home.

The only thing that brought any comfort was seeing that the sun rose faithfully every morning like a friend who never forgets a promise. It was the one thing I looked forward to: getting up so I could greet the first light as it cut across the steppes from the east. It was as if those rays were extended hands, helping me, and I welcomed them with tears.

While it took a long time for the melancholy to dispel completely, I also noticed that a certain calm was growing inside myself, an internal spaciousness I had glimpsed only in my deepest meditations. When I fixed my eyes on the brilliant orb and my eyes adjusted so that I could see the sun's outline, everything else fell away and there was only the sun, the giver of all life. The space within me grew, and I began to feel its effects not just when I sat at the top of the hill but in my daily life as well. I began to see that none of what bothered us from day-to-day was important. The unending work, the animals, the cooking and cleaning, the endless disagreements. There were reeducation sessions to attend and the communal projects we worked on: raising a new, red brick, two-story building for local government and party meetings; digging irrigation ditches for the agricultural experiments being conducted in our area; building chicken coops and barns for pigs that had been brought in from other parts of the country. When people around me became upset that projects did not go well or argued with each other, I saw them with more understanding eyes. Having seen what I had seen during my illness and knowing that nothing is permanent, I knew that none of the petty quarrels or setbacks in our work really mattered. Everything passes, everything changes.

By early summer, I no longer had headaches and my moods became less erratic. I began to feel energized instead of tired all the time, and all of life seemed to brighten a little, as if a clouded lens had been removed from before my eyes.

Gradually, gently, as the grasslands glowed a brilliant chartreuse with the first of the summer rains, I too was sprouting like a new blade of grass after a very long winter.

I was watching two eagles circling high overhead when the old woman returned late in the summer.

"Why did you burn everything?" I asked her. I used a clean cotton towel to wipe my finest burlwood bowl inlaid with silver. I filled the bowl with *suutei-tsai*.

"Those old things," she said, accepting the milk-tea with two wrinkled hands. On her left hand, she wore the silver ring with the oval turquoise I remembered from the healing. The ring looked to be very old, and I wondered how many healings it had witnessed and how many spirit battles it had been a part of perhaps even before the old woman's lifetime.

"Why did you want me to see you burn those things?" I asked. She looked up from the bowl, and her face crinkled into a smile.

"So many questions, *minee khuu*, my child," she said, amused.

Though comforted by the sweetness of the appellation, I let out a small sigh and sat down on a low stool I pulled up next to hers. I wanted answers to my myriad questions.

The old woman placed her half-finished tea on the low table and plucked a small piece of *aaruul* from the bowl I had placed in front of her. She seemed to consider my questions for a moment then began to gnaw on a corner of the *aaruul* that had been sun-dried to the consistency of old leather. Good for the teeth, the Mongolians had told us when we first arrived in the countryside. My own tea bowl cupped in my palms, I watched the old woman in her simple and obvious enjoyment of the *aaruul*. It occurred to me that if I was child*ish* with my questioning, she was child*like* in her simplicity. The peace I had observed in her on our last two meetings filled the *ger* and affected me like the sun's light; I finally relaxed a little as I waited for her to speak.

"Those were old things," she repeated. "Times are changing and people, including people like me, must adapt. When people don't believe in the old things anymore, they lose their power. The spirit world recedes." She opened her hands, palms upward, as if releasing doves into the sky. Her eyes followed their invisible flight.

"But spirits still exist?"

"Ah yes, of course they do. But people no longer have a need to talk to them, and so they trouble—and help—us less than before. Many healers have given up their helpers already. Not long ago, all known shamans in the region were ordered by the government to publicly renounce their spirit guides. I participated in a ceremony in which I supposedly told my guides to leave and never come back, but in my heart I knew that no government ceremony could drive my guides away. This is not a matter to be decided by humans who wear official clothing. Helpers always come to me when it is time for them to come, and they leave only when it is time for them to leave. I would not have been able to help you if they had not come during your trial. But they came."

"What happened to me, grandmother?"

Looking directly into my eyes, the old woman replied without hesitation. "If you had been born in a different time, you would have become a spirit-healer like me. But things are different now. Although you engaged in a spirit battle, you were not given a helper or one has not come to you yet." She turned the *aaruul* around and began gnawing on another corner. "I wish I could tell you more, but as I said, times are different now. Yours is a very different path and you need to make your own way."

"Was I not given a helper because I'm Chinese?" I asked.

She chuckled. "These categories, these human distinctions, they do not matter to the spirit world. No, it is because the world has different needs now. You have a gift for healing. You may or may not be given a choice in how you use the gift."

For several months now, I had waited for the old woman's return hoping that she of all people could bring some clarity about what happened to me. Now I saw that without the shamanic garb and without her spirit helpers, she was just an ordinary old woman chewing on some *aaruul*. She would not be able to give me any answers. "I do not feel that I am special in any way," I said. "I don't think I can heal anyone."

This only made her chuckle more. "This is true: you will never heal anyone. It's not in your power. It's not in my power either. People are only healed when they allow themselves to be healed, and it happens whether we are there to assist them or not."

She paused, looked closely into my face, then raised her hands, palms facing me, and closed her eyes. I closed my eyes too and immediately felt a soothing warmth in the center of my chest even though her hands were a distance away from my body. Tension I had not been aware of until that moment melted away, and a feeling of peace came over me.

"There will be times when you will be needed so you need to prepare yourself for the role," the old woman continued. Although she had lowered her hands, I could still feel the glow in my chest and belly. "Sometimes it is as simple as directing healing energy with your hands. Your qigong practice is helping to refine your energies and is preparing your body, heart and mind. The teacher you knew before is a great healer and a shaman though he would not have called himself that."

"You know about Shīfu?"

"How I know certain things is not important. You, too, will know things through various means. I do not know his name, but I know he is a great healer."

"He was a great master. He was killed by Red Guards." After a long pause, I added, "I was a Red Guard."

"His form has passed from this world, but he is very much alive."

Tears welled up in my eyes at the thought that Shīfu might still inhabit this world in some form or another. Although he had visited my dream only once, there had been times when I had felt *something* when I practiced qigong early in the morning or when I sat gazing at the sun. So the master was looking out for me still. It was a great relief to know that I was not alone.

I looked at the old woman with new eyes. She seemed so ordinary. Her faded cotton *deel* was like every other Mongolian woman's *deel*, and the headscarf she wore was a dull blue color—nothing fancy. When she smiled, as she was smiling now, one could see the gaps where a couple of her front teeth had been. "We are *all* very ordinary," she said with a laugh, as if reading my thoughts. "Sometimes we are called to do extraordinary things!" Her whole face wrinkled up as she cackled.

"Keep your heart and mind open. Continue doing what you are already doing. Prepare your mind and your body." She got up slowly to go. Taking my shoulders and pulling me towards her, she sniff-kissed me on the forehead as if I were her daughter. "Guidance will come when you need it. You just need to stay open to it. Have faith. Know that it is not up to you how or even whether you will be called to help others."

The old woman's visit left me more perplexed than before, but she knew that she did not need to tell me what I would eventually come to understand on my own. After she left, it took many more weeks of sun gazing and deep meditation before things started to come together in my mind.

"I think I finally understand," I said to Bayaraa one day as he helped me hang the bedding we had just washed with water we had hauled from the river. The sheets were blindingly white under the hot summer sun, and I liked the way they snapped crisply in the brisk breeze. Clean clothes, clean bedding, abundant sunshine: it does not take much for one to be content.

As was often the case with Bayaraa, he immediately understood what I was referring to. "What do you understand?" he asked.

"I was trained as a scholar, but none of what I studied is relevant now. None of the clever things I learned in school helped us after we were exiled. Our Poet. Xiǎomèi." Her letters had always been few and far in between, but I could only guess how difficult the adjustment back to city life was for her. Schools were still closed, jobs were scarce, and friends and classmates who had also been sent down to the countryside were, like me, still at their remote sites of reeducation and unable to return.

"When I was young, our neighbor was a very wise and accomplished teacher. He was a well-respected qigong master in Beijing. I could have learned a lot from him, but I was young and foolish and he sent me away. As you know, when I first came here, I was absolutely committed to doing what I'd been trained to do: love our country; build a strong society; support the revolution. None of that is important anymore. I was living for abstract concepts that were used to manipulate the unthinking masses."

"And now?"

"I've finally learned a little humility," I said with a rueful smile. "Years ago, that great teacher asked me to find what it is I need to master. I finally understand that the only thing I can master is myself. Everything else is beyond my control."

"Yes," Bayaraa said as someone who already understood what I was only just beginning to piece together. He smiled at the sheet he was holding up for me to pin. For someone so young, Bayaraa was remarkably wise, but he had spent his whole life learning from the greatest teacher of all, the natural world.

I thought about Shīfu's composure and the power he projected without effort. I remembered his humility, kindness and presence. Nothing he said or did was random or unconsidered, and he always moved from a place of inner peace even when faced with death. The old woman, too, possessed the power of a master. As ordinary as she seemed, she held herself with a grace that comes from deep wisdom and self-knowledge. Even when not engaged in healing rituals, her eyes saw far beyond physical forms, and what she saw allowed her to embrace the transitory nature of this world and to hold the preciousness of life in all its forms. It was what she showed me during the illness. I could only aspire to a fraction of the greatness that Shīfu and the old woman embodied, but having experienced their power first-hand, I had a true compass reading at last. I decided then and there to follow in the footsteps of these masters which meant, I realized, knowing and following my heart.

"Bayaraa, I don't know how long I will be here in the countryside. I still don't understand what happened to me and what it means. But I want to learn what the land has to teach me. I've gained so much living here." I kept my gaze focused on the laundry basket as I spoke, suddenly unable to look at the man who, not so long ago, I had seen only as an obstacle to my ambitions.

Bayaraa stopped what he was doing and looked carefully at my face. Without a word, he ducked under the flapping lines of laundry and wrapped me in a warm embrace.

# Malcolm's Cousin



Although a day had passed since Natalie had safely accompanied Dāndān home from the hospital, she was still trying to shake the heaviness of the experience. She could have been more attentive when she taught her evening class, or maybe it was inevitable that one of the newer students—a high maintenance, slim, but out of shape young socialite—would do something stupid like tumble theatrically out of a balancing pose, spraining her wrist in the process. Sobbing hysterically like a child, the young woman accused Natalie of being a horrible teacher and stormed out of class, collecting her friends on the way out. The loss of a student like that was a relief to Natalie more than anything else, but getting what was left of class back on track after the dramatic exit took everything she had. It was hard enough to teach class while worrying about dwindling student numbers, and now there had been an injury. Promoting her classes at the new health club in Cháoyáng had always been a challenge, but class attendance lately was lower than it had ever been. On many days only one or two students showed up or she had to cancel class entirely. The business was not going well, and she knew she would need to confer with Malcolm about it soon. He would not be pleased to know that they had been in the red for months now.

When class was finally over, Natalie left quickly without stopping to exchange a few words with the handful of students who were left. Dāndān had always been the hub of energy and light that brought all the yoga students together, and her absence left everyone at a loss. Wondering when Dāndān would be well enough to return to class, wondering if she would ever return, Natalie did not at first register that she could not find her bike until she had walked up and down the long rows of parked bikes several times. It was not until the sixth pass that she finally found the broken lock dangling pathetically from the post where her bike had been. She sighed. In the descending darkness, the road in front of the health club was a slow-moving river of steel and headlights. Dusk, painted in darkening pinks and oranges, was a pretty backdrop behind Beijing's skyline of high-rises. On another day it might even have struck Natalie as romantic. The air quality had been especially bad these past few days—the pollution index regularly shot past 400 API—but it did make for an enchanting sunset.

The city had seemed so vibrant, so energetic, so dynamic when she arrived two years ago, yet the longer she stayed the more the small things began to eat away at her. The unending rivers of human and car traffic all over the city had been a novelty during the first few months, but now almost every aspect of Beijing life irritated her. Just recently, Master Zhu had lectured her in his ponderous, didactic way about trying to see the good in every situation. There is a learning opportunity in every bad thing that happens, he had told her with a sagacious nod. He could afford to be sagely: he was chauffeured around in one of the institute's black Audis.

Natalie wearily considered her options. Taking the bus was out of the question even if she had been familiar with the routes and Chinese names of the stops. Packed to overflowing, the buses muscled their way between cars, taxis and the occasional courageous or foolhardy cyclist who ventured outside the bike lanes. Inside, the standing passengers swayed against each other, their tired faces greenish under the dim fluorescent lights. Those lucky enough to be seated stared dully out the windows or dozed, their heads bobbing up and down with the starts and stops of traffic. The subway was not an option either. She was too far from the city center and from the Second Ring Road. Although there were plans to expand the lines for the upcoming Olympics, the closest subway stop was still twenty-five minutes away by bike and she would almost be home already anyway.

It was half an hour before a taxi pulled over for her. Many Beijing cab drivers were chatty and fiercely opinionated, but this one did not say much which suited Natalie just fine. She settled with a sigh into the back seat and tried to relax. Traffic moved at a crawl. The red numbers on the meter flashed as the minutes ticked by, and Natalie lamented that she could have been home by now if she had just walked the hour it would have taken to get home. But, in the spirit of turning an unpleasant situation into a learning opportunity, she sat back and tried to follow the rapid Chinese of the *xiàngsheng* program playing on the radio. Too tired to concentrate for long, however, she allowed the words to flow over her, the audience's periodic laughter punctuating her consciousness.

In front of her apartment building at last, Natalie handed the driver a one hundred yuan note for the astonishing 86 yuan fare. She gathered up her things and waited for her change, but the driver was examining the one hundred yuan note carefully, turning it over and over and holding it up to the light. He glared at her. "It's fake."

"How can that be? I got it directly from the bank."

"I don't take fake money." He turned almost completely around in his seat, his tone becoming aggressive. Flustered and apologetic, Natalie hurriedly found another one hundred in her wallet and handed it to the driver. He examined the new bill carefully, rubbing the paper between his fingers and holding the watermark up to the light. After a ridiculously long time, he finally grunted and handed her the change through the bars of the wire cage that enclosed the driver's seat.

It was only after the taxi had disappeared into the night that Natalie realized the driver had never returned the "fake" bill. He had also not offered to give her a receipt and she had been too flustered to take down his ID or the vehicle number. Too late, she remembered that he had sized her up with cold eyes when she had first gotten into the taxi and something about his manner had made her vaguely uneasy but she had been too tired to register the feeling.

Feeling utterly defeated by the day, she just wanted to be home. Maybe Malcolm would be back and she could cuddle with him, relax into his arms. Hot tea would be nice. Overcome with a sudden nostalgia for something comfortingly American, she decided to treat herself to the spiced cider packet she had been saving for the upcoming holidays. She could heat up some apple juice she had in the fridge.

Already anticipating a long, hot shower that could wash away the unpleasantness of the day, Natalie stopped short when she walked through the door. All the lights in the apartment were on, and the first thing she saw—almost tripped over—was a pair of very high black patent leather heels in the entryway. Designer quality, not cheap Chinese knock-offs but the real thing, and very sexy. Malcolm was home and he was not alone.

They were sitting on the white couches, wine glasses held loosely in their hands. For a moment, all Natalie could think about was how difficult it would be to get red wine stains out of white upholstery.

"Ah, Little American," Malcolm said *in English*. His tone was unusually jovial. "You look tired. Take a load off. Meet my cousin from Shanghai. She is visiting Beijing this weekend." Then switching into Chinese, he turned to the woman. "Xiǎo Fēn, this is my flat mate *Nàtǎlì*." The woman smiled and extended a well-manicured hand, her eyes as cold as the cab driver's. For the second time that evening, Natalie felt herself the object of keen, shrewd scrutiny. Her face grew very hot. Malcolm had never spoken English to her before, and it immediately distanced them as if Natalie could not speak Mandarin fluently. As if they had never been lovers.

A certain familiarity in the glance that Malcolm exchanged with the woman told Natalie everything she needed to know. She was not so naïve as to believe that this woman with her flowing salon-styled curls, smart suit ensemble and, of course, the four-inch heels parked by the door, was any ordinary "cousin." There had even been a few times when Malcolm had introduced her to his friends as his "cousin" from America. It simplified things and deflected the inevitable questions, he had explained to her at the time. It had seemed odd, the evasion, but she had chalked it up to Chinese face-saving dissemblance.

"My bike was stolen," she stammered in Chinese.

"That's too bad," Malcolm said mildly, still in English. "That makes you a true Beijinger, doesn't it? Everyone gets their bike stolen in Beijing at least twice." He exchanged smiles with the woman who, like Malcolm himself, was far beyond bicycle riding. "Xiǎo Fēn and I are going to try that new Xīnjiāng restaurant in Xīchéng. Would you like to join us?"

The multiple blows of the past twenty-four hours had shattered the thick lenses that had obscured her vision for far too long—it was Malcolm to a T. The woman was exactly his type: smart, fashionable, sophisticated, wealthy. He spent more time in Shanghai than in Beijing, and the apartment here contained few traces of his life. With Natalie, he had always been fraternal, indulgent, but he had always kept her at a distance with the easy banter and evasive replies. The aloofness behind the sporadic affection, she had told herself, was due to his Chinese reserve and cross-cultural differences. She had wanted so badly for their relationship to mean something that she had ignored all the signs. But the eternal dance between lovers was pretty universal, she realized now: lack of commitment was lack of commitment whatever the cultural context.

For once Natalie did not blurt out the first thing that came to mind. She did not say to the woman, don't trust a man. Abortions are painful. Instead, she turned around and headed back out into the night. She did not know where she would go. She would move her things out later.

Beijing was decked out in full autumnal glory as the city geared up for the upcoming Mid-Autumn Festival. Red, gold and lights everywhere one looked. But Natalie was not looking as she strode up one street and down another, not caring where she was going, turning randomly. Really, there was nowhere for her to go. Three college-aged Americans emerged from a shop, bags of moon cakes swinging from their hands. They stopped laughing long enough to take in her wild hair and wooden face as she brushed rudely past them, almost knocking one of them—the Latino one—off balance. *Hey!* he said to her back, but she kept walking. On another day, she might have stopped to talk to them, her fellow compatriots. Or she might have wondered how two Black and one Latino guy fared living in China, albeit in cosmopolitan Beijing. Did locals go up to them to touch their hair or stare at their dark skin? Were they passed over for English teaching jobs in favor of fair skinned foreigners, the "real" Americans?

The college students reminded her of Malcolm's latest case. In the end, in what was supposed to be a mutually face-saving compromise, Malcolm had refused to work with an American couple. He had been so sheepish about the whole thing that it took some badgering on her part to finally figure out what the problem was: he would not help the couple adopt a Chinese baby because they were Black.

Malcolm. When they first met there had been the wolfish allure, but now she had seen the man. Would Malcolm have toyed with her as he had if she were Chinese? Or would she have understood the game better if she *had* been Chinese? Just as she thought she was beginning to understand how Chinese society worked, just as she was beginning to feel that perhaps there was a future for her here.... But she had understood everything even if she had not wanted to see. And that was the kicker wasn't it? The truth had been in front of her face all along.

She did not know how long she walked the city even after it began to rain heavily. It was not long before she was completely soaked but she did not mind—she enjoyed the earthiness and chilliness of the rain. Because she had taught back-to-back classes all over the city that day, she had not eaten since morning but she was not hungry. She relished the feeling of being empty.

After several hours of wandering in the rain, Natalie realized it was getting late and she was deeply tired. Looking around her, she saw that she was in the Cháoyáng district again. Ironically, she was not far from the health club where she had taught class earlier that evening. There was a hot springs spa up ahead where she and Dāndān had once soaked in the large communal women's pool and gotten massages. It was not uncommon for people to spend the night in such places.

The spa, modeled on a traditional bathhouse, was one of the classier ones around. It was quiet on a weekday night, and there were only a couple of older women resting their heads against the pool's edge. They did not open their eyes when Natalie entered. Natalie showered quickly then eased herself into the scalding water. As her body adjusted to the heat, she allowed herself to go completely limp for the first time that day. It felt good to be naked, unencumbered. She closed her eyes and rested her head against the pool's edge. The water gradually became still, and Natalie could no longer feel where her body ended and where the water began. Exhausted beyond thought, she finally released the illusions that had weighed her down for far too long.

*The young woman insists on carrying Wú's groceries back from the market and helps her put them away. Wú boils water to soak two peaches. They each cradle a peach in their palms and peel the skin away with ease after plunging the peaches into cold water.*

*They enjoy the bright yellow, juicy slices out in the courtyard in the early afternoon sunshine. It is pleasant to sit together in a comfortable silence that needs nothing more. Wú has shared more about her life with the young woman than she has with anyone, and the younger woman, in turn, opened up about her life since coming to Beijing.*

*She looks relaxed now, more at ease.*

# Letting Go

INNER MONGOLIA, 1972

WHEN SOMEONE STEPPED OVER the threshold of my *ger*, I knew without turning around that it was Bayaraa. One knows when a loved one is near.

"Nohoi hori!" *Hold your dogs*, he said, the traditional greeting more habitual than literal. Shīzi and Banhar had come in with Bayaraa and were eagerly sniffing his hands, *deel* and boots. Their tails were whipping up a small windstorm as they always did when he visited. I smiled seeing them. One glance at Bayaraa's face, however, told me all that I needed to know.

"Xiǎo Wú," his expression was mild but I could tell he was choosing his words carefully. "I cannot stay in town any longer—I need to return to tend the horses."

"I understand," I said. I poured him a bowl of *suutei-tsai* and offered it to him in the traditional manner, my left hand supporting my right elbow. So many things had become second nature to me in the fourth year of my exile. Bayaraa lowered himself carefully onto a low stool and rested his elbows on his knees, the bottom of his sun-bleached cotton *deel* spreading like a faded blue tent around his legs. The top three fasteners of his *deel* were undone, the flap over his chest hanging casually open, and I could see several sheets of folded paper he had stashed in the front. Bayaraa did not say anything about the papers and took his time blowing gently across the surface of the tea before taking slow, meditative sips. He focused his gaze on the creamy contents of the bowl.

I moved around the *ger* doing small things. Putting the sun-dried *aaruul* away in a cloth bag. Checking the yogurt I had made the day before. Rolling out dough I cut into thin strips for the evening's noodle soup. When two people have known each other for a time, the very silence they share is an expression of deep intimacy. Normally I relaxed when Bayaraa was near, enjoying the way his presence always made it feel as if the *ger* was filled with light. The light was muted today, however, as when clouds obscure the sun.

When I had run out of things to do, I finally spoke. "Maybe we don't need to change my residency. Or yours. It doesn't matter where we're registered. I can still join you in the countryside and help you with your work." His eyes flickered up to my face for an instant before looking down at his bowl again.

"You know as well as I do that we cannot marry without official approval. Without the proper papers, our life together would be very difficult. Everything we try to do would be many times more complicated." His face softened with the next thought. "What if we had children?" he asked. It was just a question, but I felt it as a blow to my stomach. Tears formed in my eyes while my hands continued working, mechanically cutting strips of *borts*, the jerky we had dried last winter by hanging strips of meat from the *ger*'s rafters.

I was silent for a long time. Gazing out at the gold-tinged landscape framed by the open door, I saw that the sun had begun its inevitable descent in the intensely blue sky. The dogs began to stir near the door, lifting their noses to sample the early evening breeze, ready for their sentry duties. They looked at me expectantly, but my head was filled with too many thoughts. "I can approach the Brigade Leader again," I said, but even as I spoke I knew that it would be futile. We had done everything we could in the past few years to obtain a marriage license, but we could as well have been trying to slaughter a goat with a needle for all our efforts. The fourth time we submitted our request, we had discreetly presented Brigade Leader Dorj with a very fine gelding that had taken all of our combined savings to acquire. It had been a significant gift and a pointed refusal. Some relationships are as fragile as porcelain bowls: once shattered, they are impossible to mend. Four years had passed since the incident with Xiǎomèi and Poet's death, but Dorj had never warmed to me or to any of the remaining Beijing students, and our relationship was still fraught with mutual mistrust. Unfortunately for us, she was the one person whose support we needed in order to get anything done administratively.

Bayaraa let out a long sigh. Perhaps he, too, was thinking about the many warm evenings we had ridden out past the *gers*, beyond the bend in the river. In the beginning, I had been very fearful of the open countryside at nighttime. There were wolves, the black water of the river that claimed lives, unknown dangers lurking in the darkness. Over time, however, I learned to open my heart to Nature's, and to a man's, gentle side: luxuriant summer grass made a soft bed; light evening breezes caressed our skin as sensuously as any lover; the river burbled peacefully nearby. We made love beneath the stars, in the moonlight, night breezes playing with the corners of the blanket we spread over the grass. Our horses grazed nearby as the dogs sat watch. Over the years, I learned that it was not Nature or wild animals that I needed to be wary of because I could understand their ways. It was humans who posed the greatest challenges.

"We are just two small people," Bayaraa said. "There are many things we cannot change. If we struggle against forces that are greater than we are, it will always only be that: struggling. It would be like forever riding with our faces against the driving wind and snow. *Khetsuu*. Difficult." He looked at me, at the tears streaming down my face. "One day you will return to the city," he said softly. "But you are here now."

It was getting late. I needed to attend to the animals and Bayaraa had a distance to ride while it was still light. Instead of going about our business, we found ourselves standing side by side in silence by the livestock pen, our elbows resting on the top railing as the sun slid lower and lower in the sky. The great grassland, bathed in the golden-orange light of the sunset, was spread out before us in all her late summer glory.

When I first arrived, I had been awed and scared by the vastness of the landscape that ran to the horizon in all directions. I could not appreciate its magnificence. With nothing but grass and rolling hills as far as the eye could see, I had felt very vulnerable and exposed and had yearned for protective city walls. I marveled that humans could eke an existence out of such inhospitable conditions where just getting enough water to bathe once a week was a chore that required hours of preparation. As the months turned into years, however, I began to see that the grass, the rain, and the bright sun were essential to our existence. The grassland nurtured our animals who fed us. It hid the holes of fat marmots that made juicy barbeques. In some places, it was lush enough to support a herd of thousands of animals while in other places it gave way to the poplars, birches and sea-buckthorn bushes whose fruit we juiced in the summer.

In the distance, framed by the gently undulating jade-green hills, a single rider rode towards town, his flocks meandering slowly in front of him. His solitary voice drifted over to where we stood—a song about the abundant grassland that Bayaraa had taught us that I could sing myself. The rider peered in our direction and, still singing, raised his arm in greeting. We waved back. Farther on, I could see the white speck that was our neighbor's *ger*. Women with whom I had exchanged stories, gossip, and advice in a mishmash of Mongolian and Mandarin for the past few years emerged with their milking pails and went to let the cows into the corrals where their calves were tied. I could hear the hungry bawling of the calves from where we stood. These were the evening sights and sounds of the countryside, as familiar to me by now as the face of the Mongolian man who stood next to me.

Bayaraa's horse, saddled and ready, waited patiently by his side. He dropped his golden head to nibble idly at a few blades of grass that grew around the fence posts. Then, sensing something, he threw his head up, long black mane flying, and snorted. Without looking, Bayaraa stretched out his hand, and the horse bowed his head to blow gently into the rough palm. Man and horse, horse and man. I had never witnessed a more natural pairing and suddenly found myself wondering how I ever could have thought that I might be a part of this beautiful, primal, herder's world. No matter what I felt in my heart, no matter how well I learned the language, no matter how much I had come to love the rich, green land and these hardy people, something always returned me to the reality that my place was not here. Dorj's refusal to grant us official permission to marry was only one reminder among many that I would always be an outsider. Bayaraa was right. I was a Han woman, and my place was in the city. I thought of the hurt my people had endured and knew that one day I would return to Beijing where people so desperately needed healing. Bayaraa would not be coming with me.

Yet even knowing this, because it was Bayaraa I stood next to, a deep contentment filled me as we gazed out across the pastureland that had so challenged and nourished me during my exile. There was no explaining the deep gratitude that filled my chest and settled with an ache in my throat. I did not need official sanction or even the Mongolian sky god's blessing to love. No one could take from me the vast, seamless peace I felt when I was with this man who had invited me into his world of plants, animals, spirits, and song with such sincerity and generosity. If it were not for Bayaraa, I would not have known how to heal myself.

Loving Bayaraa meant loving the grassland that had given birth to and sustained him. Loving him also meant accepting that some day she would reclaim him even as I would be called back to the city where I was born. Who could say how much time we had left together? But at that moment, my heart was full, my soul was content, and it was enough.

Finally, Bayaraa turned to me, his eyes holding a smile. "Sain suuj baigaarai," he said, as he always did. *Be well.* It was the customary phrase for leave-taking, and I understood the expression in his eyes. Then he added in Mandarin as an afterthought, "Try to stay out of trouble!" My hands tucked into the sleeves of my *deel*, I smiled back at him as he mounted and rode away.

"Bayartai," I said, and thought about the meaning of the Mongolian word for good-bye: *with joy.*

# Anthropo



NATALIE SAT FACING MALCOLM across a table spread with a pristine white linen tablecloth, but they were carefully avoiding each other's eyes. In the center of the table, a single white rose was framed by leafy green sprigs and sprays of baby's breath. Around them, well-heeled Chinese and ex-pat patrons conversed in hushed tones, their voices creating a dignified murmur that permeated the room like the slow jazz playing in the background. Three enormous chandeliers swung from the high ceiling and cast a lethargic light over the bar, the red leather-lined booths along the wall, and the pale tables in the middle. There were no windows. Anthropo was Beijing's finest European restaurant. No communal dishes, no creaky lazy Susans, no greasy, chipped teacups here. Though it was still fairly early, a few patrons were already seated comfortably on the plush sofas next to the bar, after-work apéritifs resting on low tables in front of them.

The restaurant, a cross between a gentleman's club and a smoky French bistro, reminded Natalie of the faculty club at CalTech where her father had taken her to attend a dinner hosted by a family friend, a professor. Perched on the edge of a chair that was too large for her, young Natalie had felt similarly awed and rigidly polite. Then, as now, confronted with such opulence and privilege, she had felt slightly defiant beneath the club's vaulted ceilings.

As they waited in silence for the meal to be served, Malcolm leaned back in his chair and affected the same blasé air as the foreigners though his eyes remained watchful. He had not spoken to her since they left the apartment. Her mind blank, Natalie also said nothing. Keeping her face carefully neutral, she counted the twenty tables and eight other patrons over and over so she would not have to look at him. She studied the deep red carpet that bore neat, symmetrical vacuum marks, and she noticed how crumbs fell from the mouth of a portly, half-balding foreigner when he bit into a flaky pastry. Speaking loudly with his mouth full, he did not notice the crumbs collecting on the front of his shirt. His dinner companion, a Chinese woman dressed in a slinky dark blue qípáo with a considerable amount of jewelry wreathing her neck, nodded at fixed intervals. The bright smile on her face did not vary or reach her eyes.

The restaurant had been Malcolm's choice, of course. It was open only for dinner and there were no menus: diners were served a set number of courses at the chef's discretion. After a painfully slow half hour during which they nursed their drinks in silence—red wine for him, sparkling water for her—the courses began to arrive at their table at carefully spaced intervals. Escargots à la Bordelaise, Pâté du Chef, and Saumon Fumé were followed by a thimbleful of lemon sorbet to cleanse the palate. Finding nothing that she could eat, Natalie nibbled at the vegetable garnishes and left the slippery snails, the fatty liver and the translucent salmon flesh untouched.

There was a small, expectant pause after the sorbet cups were removed, and then the waiter arrived with Anthropo's signature dish, the delicacy that gave the restaurant its name. This dish was always served regardless of what other courses appeared in the line-up, and the meat was always served bleu. It was said that Anthropo alone in the entire city of Beijing—and perhaps in the whole country—was able to secure the necessary ingredients.

When the waiter brought out two small, white plates, the simplicity of the presentation surprised Natalie: there was not even a parsley garnish for her to nibble on. She stared at the dish that people spent thousands of yuan to taste: a few thin slices of meat sashimi drizzled with a dark red sauce the color of fresh blood. Before leaving the apartment, Malcolm had told her that the cut of meat was made in such a way as to keep the animal alive. One could even say that the meat was harvested in a humane fashion.

Malcolm picked up his knife and fork and cut off a small bite of meat. He chewed slowly, savoring, his expression almost reverent.

The waiter returned to see if everything was in order and Natalie noticed with a start that he was Number 34—the young man who gave her massages at the day spa that she went to in Cháoyáng. She did not know which was more surprising: that he worked here too or that she had not noticed that it was he who had served them the first few courses. Number 34's eyes were cast modestly downward, and he gave no indication of recognizing her although they always chatted like old friends when she went for massages. Like thousands of other migrant workers who came from the countryside looking for work, Number 34 had come to Beijing a year ago from one of the northeastern provinces. A handsome, broad-shouldered young man who had not been in the city so long that he had lost either his country simplicity or, on a certain level, his innocence, he always exclaimed good-naturedly over the knots he found in her neck, shoulders and back. Natalie liked Number 34 for his frankness and cheerful sense of humor—she would almost consider him a friend—but she realized now with a jolt that she had never learned his name. The spa always referred to its attendants by number and so had she.

Number 34 withdrew after Malcolm's assurances that the food was excellent. Natalie sighed quietly then drew a sharp breath as she scanned the room for the umpteenth time. It was not inconceivable. Master Zhu rubbed shoulders with many wealthy and important people in Beijing, but she never imagined that she would see him in a place like Anthropo. His dinner companion was a young Chinese woman who looked to be barely out of her teens. Like Dāndān, she had long flowing hair and was very pretty, but even from a distance she looked like a scared, smiling little girl. Natalie sat upright and froze, as if she could avoid detection if she did not move. The last time she had gone for teachings, before Dāndān's hospital visit, he had been so pleased with her progress that he had promised her, his star student, special teachings that he reserved only for the very select. She had felt greatly honored and gratified by his generosity towards her. But Dāndān had also been a star student.

There was nowhere for her to go. She could not return to Malcolm's apartment. Trying to tamp down a rising panic, she scanned the room for a lifeline, for anything, and it was then that she saw the full name of the restaurant in sweeping, golden letters on the opposite wall. This, too, she had not noticed before: *Anthropophagie.* As was typical of a lot of signage in China, the English translation in smaller gold lettering was a little off: *The Art of Human Consumption.*

Suddenly, everything seemed off and Natalie's anxiety turned into irritation. The name of the restaurant should be *Gastronomie* instead of *Anthropophagie*, she thought pedantically. She had taken a couple of years of French in college and knew that anthropophagie meant cannibalism, not the art of eating well. "Gastronomie" would have been a much better name for the restaurant if the Chinese owners had wanted something exotic and French-sounding.

Gazing down again at the sashimi slices and the blood-red sauce that had begun to congeal on her plate, Natalie could not shake the feeling that she was missing something very important but could not for the life of her think of what it was. Without asking, Malcolm reached over for her plate and began to eat her portion. Preoccupied and still trying to avoid being seen, she did not protest, mesmerized by his chewing.

By the time Number 34 cleared away the white plates and served a light salad she could eat, Natalie had lost her appetite. She picked at the radicchio and lettuce, her eyebrows furrowed.

What was she not seeing? Awareness danced just outside her consciousness. When she glanced furtively at Master Zhu's table again, she realized that his dinner companion was a beautiful marble statue with pale, flawless skin. The portly foreigner's dinner companion was also a marble statue with her frozen smile, but Natalie was so preoccupied with trying to understand what she did not know that she was not surprised.

The cheese plate arrived. Delicate slices of headcheese gleamed next to a selection of cheeses, and it finally became very clear. The headcheese was far too fine to belong to any kind of conventional livestock animal, and there was no question about whether it had been harvested humanely or not.

Natalie stumbled for the door, clapping both hands over her mouth, but she could not keep the rotten *Táo Huā Yuán* peaches from pouring out of her onto the immaculate red carpet.

# Doors

BEIJING, 2007

NATALIE FINDS IT HARD to believe that not so long ago she had enjoyed strolling and biking around Beijing for no reason other than to explore the city. In her first year here, there had been many days when she had taken long bike rides around the city just to absorb the Chineseness of it all. Dodging taxis, cyclists, and indifferent pedestrians, she had cycled down broad boulevards and narrow lanes while the various districts of Beijing, old and new, rolled open before her like a scroll painting. Whatever they might have looked like in earlier times, the streets bordering the *hútong* districts are now crammed with shoebox-sized mom-and-pop businesses that vie for storefront space and consumer yuan: hole-in-the-wall *bāozi* joints need no more advertisement than the meat and garlic fragranced steam that beckons from open doorways; bike repair shops with their grease-stained sidewalks dotted with tiny, shiny ball bearings that roll around underfoot until they come to rest in the cracks in the pavement; flower shops live next door to jewel-toned funereal linens (Natalie had once mistaken one such place for a bedding shop and had ended up backing apologetically out the door); shops that sell baby paraphernalia just a few doors down from "adult health" shops with their strategically screened windows; pirated CDs and DVDs are cozy neighbors to hundreds of different kinds of teas. These days, with virtually everything manufactured in China, the cities are cluttered with consumer goods. Everything is sold in China, and anything can be bought. Jewelry, electronics, accessories for electronics. Real and knockoff name-brand clothing, shoes, camping gear, flimsy plastic toys. Pink shops devoted entirely to Hello Kitty merch, Walt Disney knockoffs, Rolex watches. Hannah Montana, Mercedes Benz, Justin Timberlake, Samsung, Cartier, 'N Sync, Chinese landscape paintings. Tiffany's. Tibetan turquoise. Suzhou silk and Inner Mongolian cashmere.

On one such foray, Natalie had found a beautiful, wine-colored silk *qípáo* in a small, tucked-away tailor's shop. Back home, she had frequented thrift stores and consignment shops to avoid buying clothes produced with sweatshop labor, but here tailors were a dime a dozen so she could actually find clothes that fit her petite frame. She bought the glossy sheath on an impulse, wondering if she would ever have an occasion to wear something so pretty. The one time she wore the *qípáo* was when she met Malcolm's clients.

Malcolm. She does not want to think about him.

Whatever allure Beijing had held for Natalie, it is gone now. The city Natalie walks through looks like a hooker on the morning following a long night: spent, make-up smeared, dark circles under her eyes. The troupes of orange-vested street sweepers have not yet emerged with their long-handled bamboo brooms to sweep away trash left from the night before, and the littered streets are deserted. The random small eatery aside, all the businesses are still closed, their storefronts and signs grimy with pollution even after the night's rain. When not trying to attract customers, all the shops look just as they are: tired and rundown.

Her cell phone rings. A little before five in the morning and it is Malcolm. She answers the call but does not say anything into the phone.

"Where are you?" he asks her in Chinese.

"Why would you care?" she answers in English. There is a long pause on the other end, and right before she hangs up, he answers.

"I do care. Where are you? I'll come get you," he says in English.

What she should say is *go fuck yourself*, but instead she looks around and tells him where she is.

"The yoga business is a failure. I will move my things out today," she says to him not fifteen minutes later, gazing out the passenger side window. Early morning Beijing is no better viewed from car than on foot: the gray grime on walls and window glass flies by faster is all. With both hands on the steering wheel, Malcolm keeps his eyes on the empty road and does not say anything for a long time. He clears his throat a few times but does not look at her.

He turns into a street they have been down already. "Where are you taking me?" she asks. He darts a glance in her direction.

"I don't know. Are you hungry? Would you like to have breakfast somewhere?"

"No," she says, returning her gaze to the polluted city she has tried to find a home in for the last two years.

Several blocks later he clears his throat again. "Businesses succeed and fail. It's not the business I'm concerned about," he says.

"All that you invested in the business is gone. I'm sorry." Her tone is flat.

"I'm not concerned about that," he says again as he pulls into a small residential side street and kills the engine. He looks at her, finally, but immediately looks off into the distance. "Natalie. How do I say this? You're American, I'm Chinese."

"That's bullshit and you know it," she says in English, looking him squarely in the eyes. He holds her gaze for the span of a breath before looking away. Right now, she finds it hard to believe that he was ever the confident alpha wolf in her eyes.

"I don't think we need to give up on the business just yet. It hasn't failed yet—we just need to find another way to approach it. We've come so far. I'm willing to invest more in it if...if you're willing."

"No," Natalie says, "it's over." She opens the door to go.

"Wait," he says. She looks at the hand on her arm until he pulls it back and she gets out of the car. "Natalie. Xiǎo Fēn is just a friend."

Natalie gazes up at the tall apartment buildings all around them, at the long rows of bikes, at the empty red, blue and yellow exercise equipment that only old people use. She imagines the dozens of Chinese families for whom the buildings are home, still sleeping or just waking up. Soon they will be getting their single children off to school and will prepare themselves for another long day of work in cramped shops, airless offices, government buildings. What gives these people's lives any meaning? Are they struggling merely to get by in life, or is there something else beyond the endless drive for material success? Do they find meaning in the government's propaganda or an identity in their own fierce and unquestioning nationalism, that certain cocksureness about China's place on the world stage? Are they too afraid to speak openly about love, and do they run from intimacy? She is deeply tired.

"Natalie, I do care about you." Malcolm is leaning all the way over into the passenger seat, looking up at her. She wonders how much it has taken for him to say that, a man born in a stoic generation that does not talk about love, but she feels nothing hearing his words. She is thinking about other things now. She needs to move out of his apartment, and she needs to leave Beijing. Her time is up in this city. She is moving on.

"Keep in touch?" he says, trying to keep his tone light, but his smile falters.

Despite her resolve and the deep fatigue that helps to dampen the pain, it is not easy to walk away from him, but she does. With nowhere to go, she heads for the *hútong* district in the heart of the city. The residential *hútongs* are quieter and reminiscent of a time when people were not fixated on wealth and material gain, all competing for the same resources, the same illusions. She wonders if relations between people in China have ever been simpler than they are now. Malcolm would take issue with her observation that Chinese relationships are always based on calculated interests:

people keeping tabs about what they have done for others and what others have done for them, everyone keeping careful score. Given his betrayal, how could she ever trust that what he claims he feels for her is more than convenience or manipulation?

She does not know how long she wanders around the narrow *hútong* lanes, but when she looks up she sees that she has, unwittingly, arrived in front of the grand wooden gate of Master Zhu's residence. Her feet have carried her right up to his front door. Damned subconscious.

Looking up, she sees swallows circling above his courtyard and tilts her head back to watch them. Her mother once told her that swallows in Chinese culture signify springtime, the arrival of prosperous change, the replacement of old things with new. She envies the birds their freedom. No need to find a new home, no need to think about failed businesses, no need to think about men who betray the women who trusted them.

Natalie takes a few steps back from Master Zhu's doorway so she can see the swallows better. Master or not, he has shown her kindness and helped her heal on several occasions. She does believe he is a healer of some skill though his integrity is a different matter. Why is it that so many great teachers are so flawed? Or does it make them more relatable, more human? She lifts her hand to the doorbell, her fingertips lightly grazing the small, round, black button. She wants to give him a piece of her mind, to speak up on Dāndān's behalf. But then she drops her hand and pulls out the dancing horse from her visit to Inner Mongolia. Its nose, the curve of its proud neck, its back and sides are rubbed smooth from the millions of thoughts that have set her fingers moving these past few weeks.

She puts the horse back in her pocket and turns away from the grand red doors. She takes only a few steps before she stops, however. Her fingers caressing the little horse's sides, she turns around to stand between the stone lions once again.

After some time, she turns away, her steps firmer than before. She stops in front of the much smaller and plainer door of the next compound over. The door's unpainted, weathered wood looks like it has been a part of the *hútong* for hundreds of years. It is a humble door without any sort of adornment, the kind of door people walk right past without a second thought. Natalie tilts her head up to watch the swallows gliding about overhead. As she stands there, the door opens and a middle-aged woman with a market basket over her arm appears. The woman sees her, looks closely at her, and her face crinkles into the warmest and sweetest of smiles. The courtyard behind her is a veritable jungle of plants—some in pots, some growing from the ground, some trained along and completely covering the gray walls with their bright leaves: bean, tomato, cucumber and gourd vines; squash spreading their speckled leaves over the ground; chili peppers and chives; bok-choy and mustard greens. And flowers. Flowers of every color, size and description.

The older woman's smile is so warm that for the first time in a very long time Natalie feels herself softening. She thought her yoga practice had helped her to relax. She thought she had been happy because she was in love. But it is not until the walls come crashing down in the older woman's presence that she realizes how high the defenses have been all along.

It is no wonder Xiǎo Gāng always comes to Grandma Wú's for solace. True healers for a hurting human heart are rare indeed.

"You don't know me. I don't want to disturb you," Natalie says, but Grandma Wú waves away the words. Still smiling, she steps back into the courtyard and invites Natalie to enter.

# A New Friend and an Old Friend

## Beijing, 2007

Wú gets up from the wooden bench where they have been sitting and goes over to the spot where the fledging fell this morning. It is not there anymore. She spends a few minutes looking for it in the undergrowth but does not find it. Maybe its parents carried it back to the nest or maybe it was found by a neighbor's cat. It is also possible that it stretched out its own small wings and flew home.

Wú is still thinking about the fledgling when she hears a slow, firm knock on the door. It is not Xiǎo Gāng's hurried knock, like a small, agitated mouse, and it is also not the peremptory banging of the people from the neighborhood security bureau. When she opens the door, she immediately recognizes the man's eyes although he is now in his 60s and his head is as gray as her own. She cannot help smiling when she sees that beneath very new looking black trousers he is wearing bright white sneakers. He had always worn boots in all weather and in all seasons out on the grassland.

"Nohoi hori." *Hold your dogs,* he says the traditional greeting quietly, and Wú's smile wavers a little as she remembers the wolf dogs she left behind.

"You've come," she says to him in Mongolian.

"I thought I'd better see the city before I got too old to travel."

"Nonsense. We're the same age and I'm still going strong."

"I can see that you are." They stand there smiling at each other. It feels like it has been only a few weeks rather than a quarter of a century since they saw each other last. "Are you going to ask me to come in?" he finally asks.

Though he still looks as strong as ever, Wú sees how the years have taken a toll on Bayaraa. He had written to her about the jeep accident that happened shortly after she left the countryside, but it is still shocking to see the pronounced limp. Like her, his face is full of wrinkles now, and the strong fingers she remembers so well have become gnarled like the branches of an old tree. Scars that time has left on his body. The changes, the deterioration she sees in Bayaraa's form only make him dearer to her than she would have thought possible. The closer we come to death the more precious life becomes. For one, small, fleeting moment she feels a sharp pain in her heart for what they gave up and what they lost when she returned to the city. All these years she could not allow herself to think about the man or the place where her heart had found a home. It would have been too much. Even now it feels as if a great grief is held at bay by a single, rickety floodgate guarding her heart.

But he is here now. She takes a deep breath.

"This is an old friend," she tells the young woman whose name she still does not know. To Bayaraa she says, "This is a new friend," but Bayaraa and the young woman are already looking at each other.

"I know you," she says.

"You came to our *ger* camp a few weeks ago with your friend. He was wearing a red cap," Bayaraa answers. The young woman draws something from her pocket. A small, rough carving, the sides buffed smooth and shiny. Bayaraa nods in Wú's direction, and she holds the carving out for Wú to see. Wú takes the small, dancing horse, presses it tightly between her palms, and closes her eyes. She did not know a person could feel so much joy in one day. The young woman stares as Wú draws a much older carving out of her pocket: a soaring eagle, its wings smooth and dark from years and years of living by her side.

"You have one too!" She looks from Wú to Bayaraa to the two carvings and back to Wú again. Suddenly she understands. For the first time since they met, Wú sees how beautifully she smiles.

"Grandma sends her greetings," Bayaraa says to Wú in Mongolian. "I don't think she will be with us much longer. If you want to see her you should come soon." The rolling green grassland where horses dance and play. The birthplace of her soul where eagles soar high overhead riding the thermals. Of course she will go. "As you know," he continues in Chinese, "things have changed a lot since you were there. Everything is a lot more developed, but there are still a few beautiful places left. I'll take you to them." Turning to the young woman with one of his rare smiles he says, "You are welcome to come as well."

The young woman smiles and smiles. She opens and closes her mouth but seems to have forgotten how to speak amidst her tears.

"We will both come with you," Wú tells Bayaraa.

# Acknowledgments

I am deeply blessed to be in community with the following wise women and spiritual sisters whose unwavering love and support helped me take the last steps needed to send this work out into the world.

**Carie McCoy**: I said I wanted to create more love in this world, and your absolutely joyful response was, *Let's do it!* Words cannot express how grateful I am to have you in my life as a co-creator of more healing, more love and more joy. www.CarieMcCoy.com

**Dr. Tina Schermer Sellers**: Wise elephant matriarch. I am so grateful for *all* of your guidance and support these last few years, from clinical supervision to inviting me into Inanna Rising to giving me invaluable tips about self-publishing. You are a radiant force, and the world is so much brighter because you are here. I am very excited to see what we will co-create together! www.InannaRising.org

**Dr. Rohini Kanniganti**: Gentle and fierce Bodhisattva. Words are truly inadequate. Anyone who has known you and experienced your beautiful presence will understand why words cannot describe the precious gifts you offer this world. They must be felt. Deep bow to you, sister.

**Stacy Costopoulos Smith**: There is such strength, love, and badassery beneath your grace. I am so blessed to know you and am truly grateful for our friendship. www.stacysmiththerapy.com

**Dr. Leslie Drapiza**: Yes, joyful, courageous, and telepathic sister, the magic is real, and you are a very important part of all the good that's unfolding. www.medicinalinnovations.com

**Dr. Becca Lenz**: When people talk about wisdom beyond earthly years, I think of you. You are also deeply compassionate with a huge heart and so very generous. There is a reason we ended up next to each other the first time we met, and I am so blessed to have you in my life. www.merkabaintegrative.com

I am deeply grateful to the following very special souls for their support as *Mongol Healer* came into being over the course of eighteen years:

**Andrew X. Pham**: reading a bootlegged copy of your very moving memoir *Catfish and Mandala* when I was in Thailand opened me to the idea of writing *Mongol Healer*. You provided much-appreciated feedback and encouragement for which I am very grateful. Though you've since transitioned from this plane, I know that you're receiving this thanks some way, somehow.

**Holly M. Wendt** and **Robin Perry Politan,** Bread Loaf 2018 friends and amazing writers: a very special thanks to you both for your kind and generous support. I so appreciate that you took the time to read the manuscript and provide invaluable feedback.

**Courtney Sieberling**: thank you for your encouragement and insights that helped tighten up the novel's structure. I'm excited for your novel when it comes out!

**Pamela Wei Merrien**: It has been quite a journey, sister. I am grateful for the healing that we have both experienced that allows us to care for each other as adults. Thank you for reading and commenting on a very early draft. Your insightful feedback resulted in me putting the work aside for several years but ultimately was what helped me shape it into something much more compelling and true to what I was channeling. Deep bow to you, sister. I love you.

**Imogen and Artemis**: I love you both so much. You inspired me to create the first audio reading that got the ball rolling on finally sharing this work. You are both luminous beings who are bringing so much light into the world. I am so blessed that I can witness and support your journeys as they unfold. A special shoutout to Artemis for your help with the final edit.

**Leilani Norman**: You have channeled the light and energy of this work so beautifully in your art. Your dry humor and pragmatic, can-do approach were a lifesaver in the final production sprint, and your support in this project made everything that much easier. www.leilaninorman.com

**Olga Norman**: I knew the minute we connected that you would take the design up to a whole new level. I am grateful for your vision as well as stunning execution of the cover.

**Arcane Book Design:** I could not have asked for a better experience in finalizing the paperback and hardcover designs. You were always very prompt, professional, and clear in your communications, which I greatly appreciated.

**Leo Brodie**: thank you for helping me make the audiobook a reality. It was a case of the right person, place, and time. You have been a joy to share this work with.

Finally, I am eternally grateful to and humbled by **Ulu Hoku** and **Max**, two bonded friends of the Wolf lineage who are my ever-loving Shīzi and Banhar. I know I will be graced with your embodied presence again in this lifetime.

# About the Author

Born and raised in a suburb of Seattle on the unceded ancestral lands of the Coast Salish peoples, particularly the Duwamish, Regina is a second-generation Chinese American who identifies as neurodiverse and queer. They hold a master's degree in modern Chinese literature and culture from UCLA and lived for many years in Mongolia, China, Thailand, and Hawai'i. Their Chinese ancestry and long engagement with non-Western, predominantly Buddhist cultures undergird a spiritual foundation rooted in slowing down, staying connected with Nature, and honoring collective and communal paths to healing. Regina is an Internal Family Systems therapist with specializations in sex therapy and psychedelic-assisted therapy. Their work is informed by years of classroom teaching as well as practicing and teaching meditation, yoga, and energy healing.